TT full throttle

Nicole Winters

James Lorimer & Company Ltd., Publishers
Toronto

James Lorimer & Company Ltd., Publishers acknowledges the support of the Ontario Arts Council. We acknowledge the financial support of the Government of Canada through the Canada Book Fund for our publishing activities. We acknowledge the support of the Canada Council for the Arts which last year invested $24.3 million in writing and publishing throughout Canada. We acknowledge the Government of Ontario through the Ontario Media Development Corporation's Ontario Book Initiative.

Cover design: Tyler Cleroux
Cover photo: Stephen Davison

Library and Archives Canada Cataloguing in Publication

Winters, Nicole, author
TT full throttle / Nicole Winters.

Issued in print and electronic formats.
ISBN 978-1-4594-0515-8 (bound).--ISBN 978-1-4594-0516-5 (pbk.).--
ISBN 978-1-4594-0517-2 (epub)

I. Title.

PS8645.I5747T82 2013 jC813'.6 C2013-904175-3
C2013-904176-1

James Lorimer & Company Ltd.,
Publishers
317 Adelaide Street West, Suite 1002
Toronto, ON, Canada
M5V 1P9
www.lorimer.ca

Distributed in the United States by:
Orca Book Publishers
P.O. Box 468
Custer, WA, USA
98240-0468

Printed and bound in Canada.
Manufactured by Friesens Corporation in Altona, Manitoba, Canada in August 2013.
Job #87631

For my brothers

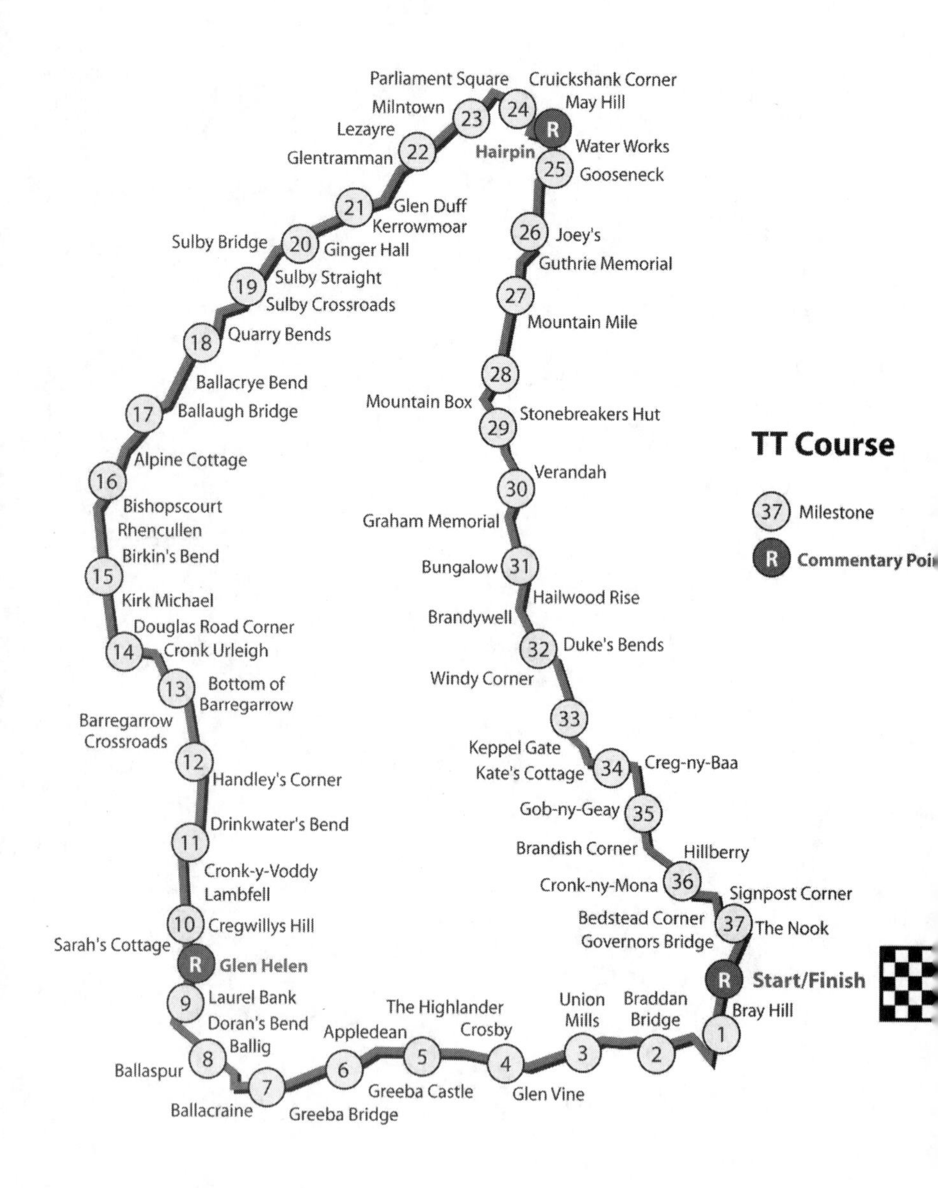

TT Course
37 Milestone
R Commentary Poi
Parliament Square
Cruickshank Corner
Milntown
May Hill
Lezayre
Hairpin
Water Works
Glentramman
Gooseneck
Glen Duff
Kerrowmoar
Sulby Bridge
Ginger Hall
Joey's
Guthrie Memorial
Sulby Straight
Sulby Crossroads
Quarry Bends
Mountain Mile
Ballacrye Bend
Ballaugh Bridge
Mountain Box
Stonebreakers Hut
Alpine Cottage
Verandah
Bishopscourt
Rhencullen
Graham Memorial
Birkin's Bend
Bungalow
Kirk Michael
Hailwood Rise
Douglas Road Corner
Brandywell
Cronk Urleigh
Duke's Bends
Bottom of Barregarrow
Windy Corner
Barregarrow Crossroads
Keppel Gate
Kate's Cottage
Creg-ny-Baa
Handley's Corner
Gob-ny-Geay
Drinkwater's Bend
Brandish Corner
Hillberry
Cronk-y-Voddy
Cronk-ny-Mona
Lambfell
Signpost Corner
Cregwillys Hill
Bedstead Corner
The Nook
Governors Bridge
Sarah's Cottage
Glen Helen
Start/Finish
Laurel Bank
The Highlander
Union Mills
Braddan Bridge
Bray Hill
Doran's Bend
Crosby
Ballig
Appledean
Ballaspur
Greeba Castle
Glen Vine
Ballacraine
Greeba Bridge

chapter 1

Hands down, British Columbia is the best friggin' backyard in the world. Endless roads overflowing with chicanes, hairpins, and switchbacks weave their way through the Rockies and fold back on themselves like ribbon candy. On either side of me, I've got these massive eight-hundred-year-old Douglas fir trees that are so big their trunks are wider than an Austin Mini and so tall I'm like a sparrow in their shadows. Whenever stuff gets to me, brings me down, all I need to do is hop on my bike, twist the throttle, and ride.

I take my turn on lead slicing up the curves. On the steep inclines I downshift and climb toward the cloudless skies, and on the downhill spirals I give the bike a break, rev low, letting 'er coast. Minus the horsepower and engine noise, this is the closest I think I'll ever get to flying. On the next straightaway, I gesture for someone else to take point, and Neil steps up. In his brown leather jacket and aviator glasses he's looking like Steve McQueen, but I know he's a hundred percent business, always choosing the smart line, flowing his black-and-silver bike and taking the apex — straightest line through each corner — with ease. My dad would have liked seeing this: Neil riding just the way he taught him.

When it's Mags's turn to pilot, I jockey for second so I can picture it being just the two of us, together. Her posture is straight-backed and flawless, and she glides her oxblood-red 650cc from side to side, curving like she's in a ballroom dance. A tiny-framed girl who handles a big bike is incredibly hot.

I just wish I knew if she liked me.

Then it's Dean on lead.

My back nearly spasms as I watch the underage punk. He's all hunched over on a motocross bike that's too small for him, and it's so beat-up you can hardly tell it's cobalt-blue anymore. The exhaust farts a trail of blue smoke and looks about ready to dump a load. Who knows where he got the thing? Hell, maybe he stole that too.

Dean heads wide into the next hairpin and starts drifting toward the gravel shoulder, and before I can figure out if he's in trouble, he's dragging his sneaker in the dirt, then shoulder-checking to watch me eat his dust.

What a scumbag. I accept his challenge.

I kick it up a notch to pass his crappy piece-of-shit bike, but he senses me coming. He starts to weave from side to side, blocking all openings. The road ahead cork-screws, and I can't pass on the outside and risk soft ground, and I'm not about to chance it on the inside near the yellow line. You never know if some jerk's gonna come the other way playing NASCAR, take his turn too wide, and make me into a hood ornament.

On the steep downward curve, Dean takes it toward the outside edge before entering the turn, hitting the apex of the bend perfectly. I twist the throttle to follow his line, then go for a pass on the corner's exit when he stuns me with a vicious front-end chop — the ultimate cheap shot. He cuts me off coming out of the turn and his back wheel drifts hard toward my front wheel. In a millisecond, twenty-two years of riding skills and experience open and close like a valve, pumping information into my muscles and nerves. I get right off the throttle and my front and back end lock, the bike sideburns and I hang on, hoping to hell that Mags and Neil aren't in my drag. To straighten out, I'm forced toward the yellow line. The next thing I see — an oncoming car.

Battleship grey.

Karmann Ghia.

Fat guy.

Eyes huge.

I'm so close I could reach out and touch the paint. I'm so close, I could take the guy's wallet.

He blasts his horn, but the sound is already fading behind me.

I see red, and the anger builds and builds until we reach Eagle's Overlook Restaurant, our planned pit stop, roughly four klicks down the road. Dean pulls in first to the parking lot. He removes his helmet and sports this shit-eating grin. I fishtail it in — not easy on a sport bike — so that a spray of gravel pelts his legs and ricochets off his bike.

"Hey, what the hell, man?" Dean yells.

I flip up my visor. "You see what he did back there?" I holler loud enough so Neil and Mags can hear. "You don't take the friggin' line like that. Jesus, I could have been killed."

Dean runs his fingers through his rat's nest of black hair and rolls his eyes like I'm some kind of baby. I get off my bike and chuck my gloves to the ground.

"What?" he says, acting innocent.

I rush him, but Neil gets in there first. He's half a foot taller than Dean and has a couple of inches on me, so he makes a good dividing wall. "Guys, guys," he says and holds his hands to his sides, palms facing out in a move we call his Jesus Christ peace pose because he once played him in an Easter crucifixion re-enactment. "Dean, what were you thinking? I told you what happened to Scott's dad."

Now I'm fuming. "Don't talk about my dad to this guy." I step around Neil and jam my finger into Dean's chest. "And you, don't ever take the line like that from me or anyone else."

At first Dean's surprised that I'm all up in his face, then his expression hardens and he swats my hand away before pulling his arm back in a half-cocked motion. I actually want him to try to take a swing. I want a good excuse to clock him.

Instead, he glances over at Neil and relaxes his stance, but not before the corner of his lip curls up. "Anything you say, Scott."

If his words were any greasier, I'd use them to lube the axle on my truck.

I shake my head at Neil. "I can't believe you even *thought* about him coming with us to the TT. You're crazy if you think you can trust him with your life."

There's a flicker of surprise in Dean's eyes. It's the first time he's heard about Neil's idea to invite him to the

Tourist Trophy Races, but the look falls from his face when he realizes the idea never turned into action. I pick up my gloves and head for the restaurant. Revenge is sweet.

Three hours later and we pull up to my place, Chateau des Saunders, a four-bedroom, two-storey farmhouse that was once my grandparents' home. My dad and I had always rented out the spare rooms in it. It's how we funded a lot of our races.

I pull past my pickup, a chocolate-brown '82 short-box I affectionately call Doris, then reach into my breast pocket for the automatic garage-door opener. The double doors rise and overhead lights flicker on. It smells of paint, metal, gas, and bike parts. It's a biker's wet dream and worth more than the house itself. Spotless, insulated grey floor coated with a waterproof seal, tools neatly hung up on walls by size, five apple-red Canadian Tire three-tier tool boxes full of wrenches, ratchets, and sockets in every size, a wall of custom-built cubbyholes, surround-sound speakers, flatscreen TV, and a space heater for working out here in winter. Dad and I used to spend countless nights tearing apart and rebuilding bikes. I park next to my red-and-white race bike. Neil comes in beside me, next to his neon-green race bike, then Mags, who doesn't own a race bike, and finally Mr. Nutsack on his piece of crap. We shut off our machines, and I remove my helmet and gloves and set them down in one of the cubbyholes by the door. Of course, Dean tosses his stuff into an empty milk crate before kicking off his sneakers and slamming the garage door behind him. How is it that his crashing on my couch for a week in January ends up as permanent? Oh yeah, Neil, this good guy who sits on my shoulder, always whispering that I should give Dean a break. Yeah, well, if the guy steals anything he's out on his ass.

Mags undoes her chinstrap and removes her helmet, and cherry-coloured curls tumble down over her shoulders. Best roommate decision ever. Aside from being hot, she's also a bike mechanic at Terry's Cycle, the largest bike shop in town. She moved in two weeks ago and took my dad's old room, which was a little hard because he died in September. But it was easier to take than having Dean move in there, like he had wanted to.

Inside, I head for the kitchen, open the fridge, and pass out some beers, letting Mags have first dibs.

"Thanks," she says. She takes the bottle from me, then gives me this big, beautiful smile.

"No problem." I was going to be all gentlemanly and

twist off the cap for her first, but I didn't. I don't know if she likes me the way I like her, and it's best to play it cool, living in the same house and all.

To show that I'm a good sport — okay, that's a lie — to continue impressing Mags, I offer Dean the only honest beer he'll ever come by until he's nineteen and can buy it himself. Of course, he says yes.

"So what do you guys want to do for dinner?" I ask.

Neil lazily stretches before slapping his abs with the palms of his hands and rubbing his six-pack, but pretending like he's massaging a spare tire. "I got it covered."

Before anyone can ask what he's talking about, there's a knock on the garage door.

"Come on in, babe," he shouts.

"Hi," Cathy hollers, and Dean *grrs* under his breath. It's what he does whenever he hears her voice. The door slams shut, and she comes bouncing into the kitchen holding a couple of grocery bags like they're pompoms. Neil picks her up before she gets a chance to set them down.

"Helicopter," he cries, spinning her around. Mags and I step back from the flight path.

Cathy squeals, making me cringe, while Dean bolts from the room. I like Cathy and her cheerleader, punch-the-air-with-positive vibes, but that voice. God. It could peel the iron off a skillet. Seriously.

He sets her down.

"I'm making burgers, yay!" she announces.

The girl loves playing domestic, and we don't mind because she can cook. I think Cathy's practising on us because, after their first year at college ends, she and Neil might be moving in together. Neil hasn't said anything official yet, but I can tell something's brewing.

Neil rests his hands on Cathy's tiny waist and draws her in close. "What would I do without you?" he asks.

"Starve," she replies, like it's obvious, and they start making out, full tongue-on-tongue action. When Mags catches me looking at her, I can feel my face grow hot.

From the living room stereo comes a sudden blast of thug music.

"Okay, okay!" Dean yells out. "Don't nobody get your panties in a twist."

The volume lowers to zero fast, but it's too late. He's broken the sacred house rule: Thou shalt play only rock and roll. He must have committed the crime yesterday when we were all out and he'd come home from the night shift at the cannery.

I head into the living room. Dean's sitting cross-legged on the buckled hardwood floor with his back against our old snot-green couch. He's got a beer beside him, an unlit smoke in his mouth, and is strumming his guitar.

Neil removes the offensive MP3 player from the stereo. He scans my dad's massive vinyl collection that spans the wall in six milk crates high and fifteen across, and selects a Rolling Stones record, showing it to Dean. "Now *this* is what I'm talking about." He slides the album out of its sleeve, places it onto the turntable, and carefully sets the needle down onto the spinning vinyl groove.

Guitars rumble and Mick Jagger starts wailing. Neil begins lip-synching about the lack of satisfaction and I imitate Keith Richards on air guitar. Dean stares at us and I can tell he's dying to make a crack about our old-fart taste in music, probably something about our being geezers gumming Jell-O, but he keeps his mouth shut. The guy's not dumb, I'll give him that. I'm surprised that for someone who can play guitar he has such crappy musical taste. Dean gets up off the floor and gives us a high-pitched Michael Jackson "hee-hee," along with a crotch grab, and heads outside for a smoke.

"Hey, pop in the TT game," I say to Neil and scoop up one of the controllers from the coffee table. I offer it to Mags. "You wanna play?"

"Sure," she says, and when she takes the wireless remote from me, her grease-stained fingertips — a hazard of being a mechanic — brush mine, making sparks shoot along the back of my hand.

Neil squats down in Dean's old spot and Mags sits beside me. Cathy takes command of the kitchen, clanging dishes and searching through utensil drawers. We choose our game players. My guy wears red-and-black leathers, my actual racing colours. Neil's guy is green and Mags's is purple. The TV screen shows an overhead shot of the Isle of Man where the Tourist Trophy Races takes place. The lap, thirty-seven and three-quarter miles (or roughly 60 kilometres — but they go by imperial), runs all the way around the small island nestled in the Irish Sea. It's the land of the Manx people, whose laws hark back to the Viking days — no joke. The race is real too. Go look it up.

"Four months and two weeks till we're there," I say, grinning big. Neil holds up his palm so I can slap it.

Saying you're going to race in the Isle of Man Tourist Trophy, or simply the TT Races, is like saying you're taking on The Dakar, the Tour de France, or the Vendée Globe. It's expensive, you need skills, tons of gear, and you have to study the course like your life depends on it, because it does. Just getting through practice week is considered an accomplishment. My dad, Neil, and I had worked our asses off to get invited to the TT, partaking in Ireland's North West 200 and securing our Mountain Course Licences from the Auto Cycle Union based on our racing CVs. The TT is the Holy Grail. Sure, the Ulster Grand Prix may be the fastest race in the world, but they say you're not a real road racer unless you've ridden the TT — the most dangerous.

"I am incredibly jealous," Mags says. "I've always wanted to head-wrench a race like that."

"Come with," I say. "We could always use an extra pit crew." Neil's cousins, Vince and Marco, from Vancouver, are our mechanics and they're okay. Neil assures me that they can do the job, but they're motor heads — guys who like to tinker with cars. Let's just say that they do work on bikes, but it's not their first love.

Of course, I'd rather have Terry in our corner backing us up, because I've known him all my life and he's like family. But ever since my dad died in September, I haven't seen or heard much from him.

"Yeah," Neil agrees. "Come with."

"I wish," she answers. "I seriously doubt Terry would let me go. I just started working for him."

Neil thinks I can't see him looking at me when Mags mentions Terry's name, but I can. I glide my rider up to the starter's line under the archway, narrow enough for one bike, and wait for the countdown to commence. "Hey, Neil, when's your new race bike getting here again?"

"Next Saturday," he says. "After the race at Goodman's — where I'm going to beat your ass on the track."

"Bah," I cry. "Strong words, little girl." Mags elbows me for that and I laugh, nearly missing my start time. My rider takes off, flying down Glencrutchery Road.

"I need a volunteer!" Cathy calls from the kitchen.

Neil and I don't move; her timing sucks.

"Coming," Mags says and gets up off the couch.

"Bray Hill," I say out loud to help Neil and me familiarize ourselves with the course. Did I mention there are more than two hundred bends in one lap? You can't mind-map this race like you can a two- to three-mile circuit with ten to thirteen turns like the one at Laguna Seca. That's why this is the ultimate road race. It takes a long time to learn it — like an average of three years — before you can even consider a podium finish. Just making it through qualifying week and getting a chance to race is our goal. To qualify, you have to come in with 115 percent of the third-fastest riders' lap during practice week. This isn't a circuit where you ride a few laps in the morning, then race that afternoon. They give you a week. So if the fastest lap time is say, I dunno, 17 minutes, and the third-fastest guy is 17.20 minutes, that means your lap has to come in at 23 minutes or you don't make the cut. Easier said than done. Just because you get accepted doesn't mean you'll get to race.

"I'm going to ask Mags if she'll help strip my new bike and get it race-ready," Neil says, waiting for his countdown so his rider can head out.

My eyes are fixed to the screen as I reach the bottom of Bray Hill and head toward Quarter Bridge. "What about your cousins? Aren't they doing that?"

"They're swamped. They asked me to get someone to do the bulk."

A small shot of something rushes through my chest. It's not adrenalin. It's more like when you sense a crack in the plan. "Braddan Bridge," I announce. "Do Vince and Marco even want to go to the TT? 'Cause if they don't, we need to know now."

"Yeah, yeah. They'll be fine. They're just swamped. There's a big car rally in two weeks. They're both working overtime."

I ride toward Union Mills and my chest floods with a second shot of whatever it's dispensing because I realize I've never been in a race with another mechanic before. All my life it's always been me, my dad, and Terry.

"Coming up to Bray Hill," Neil says as he sets off from the start.

Mags and Cathy come back into the room. Mags sits beside me, picking up the controller again.

"Neil, can you come start the barbecue?" Cathy asks.

"Yup — Quarter Bridge," he says, but his eyes remain on the screen. As I come out of Union Mills into Ballagarey, he's heading for Braddan Bridge. "Give me a sec, babe?"

Cathy takes a seat on the armrest. "So is this where you guys are going, for real?"

"Yup," I say. "Crosby Straight." I gun it down the fast stretch, passing the Crosby Pub on my right.

"Gah!" Mags cries, and I look at her rider on the multiscreen. She's ridden down Bray Hill and has successfully negotiated the right-hander at Quarter Bridge, but now she's panicking and presses random buttons. She's completely messed up the easy left-hander before Braddan Bridge, and we watch as her rider ends up in the churchyard. Spectators scatter, making all of us laugh. Thank god she's a better mechanic than a gamer.

"I kinda don't get why you want to do it so badly," Cathy says.

Her words make me shudder. How could you not want to do this? I think.

"Union Mills," Neil says.

Mags curls a lock of hair behind her ears. "Well, the idea is to pit your skills against the toughest road race course in the world."

"Greeba Castle," I announce. "Wait, is it Greeba

Castle or Greeba Bridge? I always get 'em mixed up."

"No, you had it right. Think: all castles have bridges. So, Greeba Castle, Greeba Bridge."

"Nice."

"See," Mags continues, "unlike a regular race course where there's plenty of kitty litter to slide into if you spill, there's no runoff over there. You're racing on actual roads. You have to watch for street furniture: houses, storefronts, telephone poles, railway tracks — yeah, they actually have a train on the island — stone walls, people's living rooms. One wrong move and it's game over."

I shoulder-check to look at Mags and my heart beats a little faster. By the shocked look on Cathy's face, I think hers does too, but for different reasons.

"Ballaspur." I tilt my controller hard to one side as I enter the bend that starts the head up north.

"Greeba Castle," Neil says.

"Imagine a thirty-seven and three-quarter mile or sixty-kilometre stretch in downtown Vancouver," I say. "Then throw in a few hundred bends and turns, add a set of train tracks, a mountain, and a bunch of sheep."

We all chuckle at that last part.

"Now forget going the speed limit of 40 mph, try 180 mph."

It's quiet as we watch the screen for a few minutes.

"Coming up to Ballig Bridge."

"What's 'no runoff' mean again?" Cathy asks.

I'm surprised by her lack of knowledge. Don't she and Neil talk? She should know by now what the risks are of dating a motorcycle racer. Doesn't she know how my dad died? "It's an empty patch of space where if you spill, you don't crash into anything," I say.

It gets quiet again.

"Neil, can you help me with the barbecue?"

"Sure, hon." He puts his player on pause just past the Crosby Straight and gets up off the couch, then the two of them head outside. Mags continues to watch me play. It's a tight right-hander coming into Laurel Bank and after that, a tricky twisty section. "Coming into Glen Helen," I announce. "I'm one-quarter of the way around the course."

Mags shakes her head and smiles, impressed. "Unbelievable. You're only one-quarter of the way there. I don't know how you're supposed to remember all this during the race."

"Lots of practice," I say, "and miles of luck."

Outside we hear Neil and Cathy's murmured voices.

chapter 2

No one signs up for the TT to build a reputation in circuit racing because it's a totally different skill set. It's like trying to be a tennis pro but practising on a squash court. You're not riding a closed, controlled two- or three-mile track a dozen times. The TT is on regular roads so narrow that riders have to head out one every ten seconds. The other big difference is that you race against the clock, not someone else. Pro-circuit guys won't do the TT. It used to be part of the Grand Prix Championship schedule until 1976, when top riders joined Giacomo Agostini in boycotting it because it was too dangerous. That says a lot.

My alarm goes off at six-thirty. I haul myself out of bed, take a whiz, toss on some sweats, and head downstairs to meet Neil. I can hear him shooting hoops in the driveway — total morning person. Before I leave through the garage, I stick my head into the living room. Over the past couple of days, we've been transforming the space into TT headquarters. Topographical maps and course charts line the walls; the coffee table's piled high with books, papers, road and course bend names, lap times, and race rules and regulations. I have an old TT course book from 1952 — from my dad's collection — that sits on the fireplace mantel. Our video game and the on-line videos are a million times more accurate, but it's nice to have a bit of Dad around. It tears me up that he can't be here. It was supposed to be the four of us going: me, Neil, my dad, and Terry. My dad and Terry used to talk about the TT when me and Neil were kids: "The TT — the oldest and toughest road race in the world. There's nothing like it." We'd been planning this trip for years and got serious about it after my dad turned forty-five. They don't just let anyone in who applies for the TT. Race officials take into account your previous races and times, and your reputation. I guess they deemed us worthy.

I head outside through the garage and see Dean's motocross bike stripped down to its frame with its guts strategically placed in the same way a surgeon would arrange his instruments during an operation. Good on

Mags for convincing the guy to let her give it a serious tune-up. Now if only a city garbage truck would back into my driveway and haul it away.

It's nippy out and too early for small talk, so Neil and I just get going. We start down Nestleton Road for about half a klick, our running shoes slapping against the pavement as the sun climbs its way over the mountain. When we reach the ocean, the sun peeks out from the clouds and bathes everything in an orange glow. The four-kilometre dirt trail runs along the coastline and I slip in behind Neil so that he's on lead and I can look at the sea. The Pacific's a deep blue this morning and there are a couple of thirty-foot fishing boats out there pulling in their nets. They've been up and out for hours. Hell, it's practically lunchtime to them.

I check my pulse: 149 beats per minute, roughly seventy-five percent of my maximum heart rate, which is good. I'm going to have to maintain peak effort when I'm at the TT.

The trail merges onto a paved scenic lookout and picnic rest stop. When I hit the asphalt, I kick it into high gear and leap up onto a picnic table, running along the bench part, then hopping down to fly past Neil. Now it's my turn in front. We run until we hit another tourist stop, Breakwater Cove, and high-five the metal sign that warns us of ducks crossing before we turn around and head back.

On the way home I pick up the pace and imagine I'm trying to lose Neil in a breakaway, but he stays on my heels. He takes it up a notch on the final stretch so that we're now running side by side. It's muscle versus muscle as each of us eggs the other on. I'm working it so hard my heart's thumping in my ears and my lungs are burning like a brush fire. I have to really give 'er and push through the pain because I can't let Neil win. When I hit the driveway first, he tries to fire off a long string of filthy words between breaths, which makes us both laugh because he rarely swears. We pace in small circles for a bit, sucking in sharp, fast breaths. I'd collapse on the front lawn if it weren't for all the mud patches. I tilt my upper body skyward to open up my chest and take in more air. Neil bends at the waist, putting his hands on his knees. His stomach and shoulders heave.

He slaps me on the back. "Loser showers first," he says, then sprints for the door.

I come back with a "Yeah? Loser also does breakfast dishes," and then imagine how funny it'd be if I used every dish just to see the look on his face when he came down to eat.

I head inside and find Mags sitting at the kitchen

table, reading a bike magazine, eating toast with jam and drinking tea with two fingers of milk, just like always.

"Hey," I say and pour myself a glass of water.

"Hi, Scott."

I drink down big gulps between breaths, then drag the back of my hand across my lips. "Dean's bike is coming along nicely."

"Yeah, I'm going to pull the head and do a re-valve job on it tonight."

"Good. Maybe the exhaust will stop killing birds, babies, and old-timers."

A smile plays at the corners of her mouth. "I'm a sucker for neglected bikes," she says. "I have this compulsion to rebuild them and make them hum again."

Now I wish *I* owned Dean's crappy bike.

I take out some eggs, butter, and an onion from the fridge. "Want an omelette?" I know she doesn't, but I still ask.

"No, I'm good." She flips the page to a full spread of the latest race bikes. "Hey, what got you guys into road racing? I mean, it's not like there are a lot of races here in North America to compete in."

"I know, right? We totally have the open space and the perfect terrain. I'm surprised there's not more than just track and motocross. It doesn't make sense. We did Ulster GP last year."

"Nooo," she says, and I smile, but before I can elaborate, the phone rings. Since I'm close, I grab it.

The voice on the other end is unmistakable, even though I've only heard it once, the second night Mags moved in. It's the way he clips his words in that Toronto-speak, that "can't waste time because I'm a busy businessman, so your attention to this matter is imperative" way of talking.

"Yeah, sure, she's right here." I pass the phone over. Mags mouths, "My dad?" I nod and she looks grim. Frig, I think. If I had been more on the ball, I would have warned her first and taken a message. Too late now.

She pushes her plate away and when I hand off the phone, her fingers brush mine, and the sparks ignite again.

"Hi, Dad."

I motion to see if she wants me to leave and she shakes her head, so I get started on breakfast.

"Why are you calling so early? ... Yes, it is, it's seven-thirty in the morning here. We're three hours behind, remember?"

When I take the frying pan out of the stove's bottom drawer and then close the drawer, the damn thing squeaks. I gently set the pan down onto the burner.

Mags twists the phone cord around her middle finger. "Silly? I wouldn't call what I'm doing silly. I've got a job … yes, as a mechanic … why is that ridiculous? You didn't think it was ridiculous when I worked at Motorcycle Werx all through high school."

I fast-chop some onions and throw them into the pan to let them sweat in a little butter. I try not to listen in on the conversation, but I can't help it. She paces the floor.

"No, you just want me to do what you want …"

I'm not sure if I should turn on the overhead fan, so I crack open a window, letting cool April air waft in. It fills the room with the smell of muddy backyard.

"I already told you, I'm not going back to school."

I break and separate a half-dozen eggs, keeping the whites only, then add some salt, pepper, and paprika before whisking.

Then Mags utters the kind of noise you hear from parents who are fed up with their kids tearing around the SafeMart.

I pour the eggs into the pan and they flow in and around the onions.

"Huh-uh … huh-uh … huh-uh. Yup. Whatever. I gotta go. Fine. Yes. Bye, Dad."

She slaps the receiver in its cradle. "God, I can't believe him."

I look over. "Can't believe what?"

She tsks and shakes her head. "Forget it. I don't want to talk about it."

"No problem," I say and go back to my breakfast.

She crosses her arms in front of her chest. "Why can't they get it through their thick skulls that I don't want to get an Economics degree from the University of Toronto just because they did? The whole reason I quit after the first semester and moved to the other side of the country was because I couldn't take it anymore. 'Economic theory of this, baseline statistics of that …' God. Do you know what I want?"

I shake my head, but I want to know. This is the most she's said about herself since she moved in.

"I want to be a pro mechanic for a MotoGP or Formula One racing team. Is that too much to ask for? Is that a stupid dream? Just because I'm a girl, I can't do it? What is this, the 1950s?"

I go from shaking my head to nodding my head to shaking it, then force myself to stop.

"They loathe that idea." She makes air quotes. "'It's not a *real* job,'" she mimics. "But it's my life. What's wrong with carving my own path and doing something that makes me happy?"

"Nothing," I say and find myself being drawn into her big green eyes. I fight the urge to pull her into my arms so she can rest her head on my shoulder as I tell her that it'll be alright. She continues looking at me with this spark in her eyes, and I feel a kind of energy surging between us. I half wonder if I should reach out my hand and go for it, but then Dean stomps into the kitchen, killing the moment. Mags collects her dishes, dumps them into the sink, and leaves. Dean scratches his nuts and mutters something before reaching for the cupboard and pulling down his Apple Jacks. He shoves his fist through the box top and grabs a handful of cereal, dumping it into his cake-hole. Then he opens the fridge, picks up the milk container, and drinks from the bag. What a goof.

Ferber's Fish Cannery: slaughterhouse for both man and fish. Me and about a dozen other guys stand there in our hairnets, gloves, and bloodied aprons staring at the conveyor belt as it presents us with freshly caught Pacific Chinook from behind a curtain of wet rubber strips. I switch the carving knife from my left hand to my right hand and press the handle into my palm, hard. Being ambidextrous helps with the monotony, I guess. What can I say? It's a job.

Some of the fish still wriggle and flip-flop down the line, and I take hold of a good eighteen-pounder and slap it onto my cutting surface. I raise my knife to shoulder level, do a figure eight in the air and bring it down to slice off the fish's head and tail. Then I make a clean cut across the length of its belly. I push all the useless parts into a metal trough between the belt and my cutting surface, then toss the fish back onto the belt. I knock my knife twice on the board to clean off the guts.

Our eight-hour shift finally ends when three sharp blasts boom over the PA and fish stop coming down the line.

"Thank god," the guy beside me mumbles, and soon there's a chorus of rubber gloves stretching and snapping off sweaty hands. The sound always reminds me of those cheap firecrackers Neil and I used to buy as kids from the dollar store.

I look across the cannery floor and spot the juvie head case coming my way. Dean's never hard to miss in his BC dinner jacket, unlit smoke hanging from his lips, and sans apron and hairnet, despite the rule about having to wear them on the floor. You'd think for a guy with a criminal history, he'd be grateful for having a job.

He comes over to me, grabs a low-hanging pipe that juts out of the concrete wall, and does a pull-up. "So, you seen the bossman yet for your performance review?" I shake my head. By the way Dean spits out the words, "performance review," I take it he's had his. "Yeah, well, Russ says if I don't increase my pro-duc-tivi-tee, I'm expendable. Asshole." On his third chin-up, he grimaces and his cigarette rises, brushing the tip of his nose. "You know, someone should torch this place. Ain't that right, Russ?"

I look behind me, expecting to see the boss, but he's not there. He's across the floor, outside his office, staring at us, though.

"Dean, get the hell down from there!" he barks.

Dean removes one of his hands and hangs there like a monkey. "Hey, Russ, you want to make a bet? Twenty says the Canucks kick the Leafs' ass tonight."

Russ dismisses him with a wave. "Go home before I put my boot to yours." He then hoists his pants up in a see-saw motion only to have them dive for cover under his gut when he lets go.

"Scott," Russ says. "I need to see you in my office."

Dean jumps down and heads for the lockers. "Later, sucker," he says.

I walk over and enter Russ's office to find him sitting behind a gunmetal-grey desk flanked by mismatched filing cabinets. Stacks of manila files are all over his desk along with four dirty-looking vending-machine coffee cups that resemble racetrack-marshal outposts. One of them has been there so long a green furry island is floating in it. On the windowledge, a skinny yellow plant struggles to survive in a faded margarine container.

"Shut the door," he instructs, and I do what he says. Then he gestures for me to take a seat. I look down at the chair, and it's got a big rip in the vinyl seat from ass to crotch and dirty yellow foam trying to birth its way out. Russ reaches for a file that I figure is mine, and his eyes scroll through the pages inside, the same way my grade-three teacher's used to. I half expect him to pop the cap off a red pen and start circling mistakes and then tell me that if I hand in one more book report on motorcycles, I'll get a D.

"So how you doing, Scott?"

"Fine."

"There's been some reports of people getting their lockers broken into. You missing anything?"

I shake my head. "Nope."

"Seen anything suspicious?"

It doesn't take a genius to guess that he thinks it's Dean behind all this. "No, I haven't," I say, because it's the truth.

Satisfied, he folds his hands and sets them on top of my file.

"You've been working here a while, Scott."

I nod. I've been working part-time at Ferber's since I was sixteen to save up race money. I started out with washing floors and cleaning vats, then moved onto unloading hauls and gutting. It was Neil who talked me into working full-time back in October a month after my dad died. Line work isn't exactly a career job, but I skipped out on college, and all I'd been doing at home was sitting around and turning into a bum.

"You know your dad and I once worked on the line together when we were in high school?" Russ continues. "It's a crying shame what happened. He was a great guy. Talented as hell." Russ's eyes start glazing over as he gets sucked into some memory I'll never be a part of. I squirm in my chair, widening the rip and say nothing. Silence hangs in the air until it becomes dense and awkward.

Russ clears his throat. "You're a good worker, Scott. Your productivity's good. And you've got a good attitude. I think you could be management material one day. How does that strike you?"

I muscle up something that could pass for a smile. No way in hell that's happening.

Russ settles into his chair, and when he cups the back of his head with both hands I see two yellow pit stains yawning at me. "Who knows," he continues. "Work hard and maybe you'll even take my job."

The thought of being a lifer in this place makes me want to grab a fifteen-pounder off the line and slap him with it.

chapter 3

Neil, Mags, and I arrive at Goodman's Raceway just after sunrise for the first circuit race of the season. We'll be getting in as much track time as we can before we head to the Isle of Man in seven weeks. While Goodman's isn't very helpful to a road racer, it's better than nothing. There are no road races around here. It's not like Europe where the sport is common and people are used to closing down roads for the day. Sure, we have road rallies, but those are for cars, not bikes.

Good ol' Goodman's. It hasn't changed in years. They still have the faded billboard, and old gap-toothed Brenda still collects entrance fees. In the middle of the grandstand the announcer's booth stands like a shack on stilts. Neil and I have been coming here since we were six. We met in line for hot dogs and became instant best buds. We were celebrating our first race — the PeeWee category — which consisted of one whole circuit lap. Man, those were the days, when a three-mile course felt more like 103. So while Goodman's is no longer a challenge, and a bit of a dump, it still holds a lot of good memories.

I pull the truck into the paddock and search for a place to make camp for the day. I score a sweet spot beside a tree for some late-afternoon shade and back Doris in. It's six-thirty in the morning and already the guy next to us is jetting his 125cc two-stroke. It sounds like a little kid imitating an engine into a loud speaker, *wing-wing-wwwinnnnng.* Thank god we live thirty-five minutes away, because it would suck to have to wake up to that on race day. I bet the guy went to bed after midnight and picked up again an hour ago.

I place my foot onto the back wheel to help me step up into the box and untie the ratchet straps holding down the race bikes. Neil unhooks and lowers the tailgate and slides out the loading ramp. Mags sets our extra-large Tim Horton's coffees and her tea on top of the roof and hauls her tools and equipment from the back of the cab. Dean's at home — sleeping or setting the house on fire — and Cathy said she'd meet up with Neil later.

Most of the morning gets eaten away with setting up our paddock, registration, getting our bikes checked over and approved at the mechanical inspection, and running a few practice laps. After lunch, we ride the qualifiers for the senior pro class — two fast laps — which we easily pass and secure front-row positions in the starter's grid. Like I said, this circuit's a cinch. It's the Isle of Man's thirty-seven and three-quarter miles course that takes three years to learn that's the tough one.

With time to kill before the final race of the day at 4 p.m., we chill out at base camp, listen to music, and polish the bikes. Neil chats on his phone with Cathy and makes smoochie noises.

When the rider in the paddock across from us returns from his practice run, he walks alongside his bike instead of riding it — not a good sign. He lifts up his visor.

"Keeps under-braking," he shouts to his mechanic. "Something's wrong with the brakes."

The guy glances over at us and nods at Mags like he knows her.

"Hey, Pete," she says back. Mags hasn't been working at Terry's for very long, but she seems to know everyone with two wheels.

Pete's mechanic, a small stalky guy with hair in a tangled mess and grease-stained overalls, shakes his head. "I checked everything. Put new brake pads in, bled the system, adjusted the lever, you name it."

Pete removes his helmet. I'd say the wrinkles around his eyes put him in his mid-forties. "Hey, Mags, got a sec?" he asks.

"Yeah, sure, Pete."

Both of us walk over. Their paddock smells like oil, mud, and grease.

"I'm using normal-braking markers," he says, "but I have to hang on the brakes more than normal and it doesn't seem to be able to haul it up."

She motions to the mechanic. "Start it up." He does, revving the engine a few times. Mags tilts her head to one side, her ear facing the machine. "Idling a bit high," she notes.

The mechanic nods. "I haven't been able to get it any lower."

She pulls a pencil from behind her ear and uses it to secure her hair back in a bun. The engine is cut and she crouches down, giving the brakes a once-over. When she and the mechanic don't find anything, they move on to the carburetor.

Pete and I stand back and watch the two of them work. I keep my mouth shut because I'm curious to see how Mags handles herself. This is going to sound sexist, but usually the prettier the girl, the less competent a mechanic she is.

"My guess is that it's the vacuum-release plate seals," she says.

The mechanic gives her a skeptical look, then shakes his head as if he's giving up. "Why not?" he says. "Can't hurt to check."

I watch Mags become absorbed in her work. I can totally picture her working crew for a top team, maybe with Honda or Ducati. Yeah, Italy. I can see her rocketing down the Autostrada. So what the hell is she doing in hick-town Ferber?

After some disassembly, it turns out the release-plate seals on the flat slide carbs were damaged, and they were letting air pass through whenever the throttle was shut.

"I never would have guessed it," the mechanic admits.

Pete raises one eyebrow at me like he's complimenting me on my friend, no, girlfriend. I give him a slow smile as if to say, yeah, she's hot and she's with me.

When they fire it up again, the idle speed adjustment is restored. The guys are all smiles. Watching how she diagnosed the symptoms in one area and figured out the cause in a totally different area reminded me of the micro-to-macro approach Terry used to take. No wonder word has it that Terry considers her one of his best mechanics.

We head back to our paddock. Neil is finally off the phone and has just polished off his second coffee for the day. If he drinks any more than that, he gets too jittery and starts squeaking like Cathy.

"Hey, Scott," Neil asks me. "You wanna ..." With his finger he makes air circles to see if I want to do a walk-about in the paddock and say hi to the regulars. I say no to Mr. Social. I haven't seen a lot of these people since my dad's funeral and I want to maintain my race head, seeing as how it's the first event of the season and all. I tell him that I'll talk to everyone later. Mags goes with Neil, and I head for the grandstand to take in a few junior races. On my way over, I pass by the ice-cream stand and Burt's Chippy Truck and wonder what it is about the greasy stench of cooked meat, fried potatoes, and burning rubber that says, *I'm at the races.*

In the bleachers, I take a seat on one of the metal benches and pull a program from the inside pocket of my racing leathers. There are a lot of names in the booklet I recognize from years in the sport, and there are some I don't. I stare at the list of newcomers. Half these guys won't make it through their first season, let alone the steep climb up the ranks. Young pups go into Supersport expecting to reach the top in a few years like they're the next Valentino Rossi or Jorge Lorenzo, or something, but that's rare. People think we race because we're speed junkies. While that's kind of true — the feeling *is* better than sex — this is a thinking-man's sport. Everything's coming at you so fast and you have to stay cool and collected while processing all the information you can to make the best decision. That's where the real rush comes in. Couple that with racing on city streets, like on the Isle of Man, and it's no wonder they call the TT the Mount Everest of road races.

Two hours later over the PA, I hear the announcer say, "First call to the grid, pro 600." Tiny hairs rise on the back of my neck and my heart starts pumping in one of those ring-a-bell-and-salivate reactions. I catch myself grinning.

I head back to the pits and shake the tension out of my arms, flicking my wrists and making fast fists like I'm snatching something invisible. Mags has got Doris's stereo cranked with AC/DC's *Thunderstruck*, which gets the adrenalin flowing nicely. Mags wipes her hands on her tool rag before shoving it into her back pocket, and when she sees me, she smiles.

I see Neil walking up the lane and he's got Cathy with him. Their arms are wrapped around each other like actors in a chewing-gum commercial. My dad met my mom at a track. Not here, though. They met at Donington

Park. She was an American model hired by the MotoGP Series to tour the race circuit and stand around in just about nothing all day. Their one purpose is to promote the sport, add some glamour, and if it distracts the competition, then that's a bonus too, I guess — it sure worked on my dad. When my mom found out she was preggers with me and wanted to give me up, he got her to sign over parental rights and cut her a cheque not to come back. She took it — apparently she had big plans of making it in Hollywood and I guess having a kid slows you down. Last I'd heard (from a guy who knows a guy) she's living in Sturgis, South Dakota. No skin off my nose. I've never even met the woman and I'm not interested either.

I sit on my bike, put in my earplugs, and slip on my helmet, ensuring that the strap is snug. I slide on my gloves and slap my leather palms together hard, so they make a hollow popping sound.

Cathy throws her arms around Neil's neck, pouts, and looks mock-sad and worried. God, if my girlfriend gave me that look before a race, I'd tell her not to come. I don't need a snapshot of that branded inside my skull. She follows it up with a big, sloppy kiss and a full-body hug. I think some girls are into guys like us because of the whole speed-danger thing, which you'd probably agree is friggin' awesome because it gets you laid, but when you think about it, on an extreme level, girls being turned on because we play with danger is kind of creepy. I watched my dad get dumped by a woman just because he wasn't having a good race year. You also don't want to date a girl who hates that you ride either. Before a big race you're mentally and physically trying to peak, and the last thing you need is her going on about how dangerous bikes are. The key is to find someone who doesn't hate it, but isn't trying to climb the leader-board, or is obsessed with only dating number one.

"Okay, guys," Mags says. "You're good to go."

I fire up my bike and rev the engine in steady beats before giving Neil a look that says, *Get ready to have your ass handed to you.* His freshly kissed expression falls away. Best friends or not, a race is still a race.

The two of us ride along pit lane, joining the other three-dozen riders in the pre-grid area. The stands are packed now and even though I can't hear the announcer, he's doing the roll call, telling spectators who we are and what number we're wearing.

One of the marshals gives us the okay and lets us onto the track for a few warm-up laps. Most of the riders take wide exaggerated arcs in the corners, trying to create heat on the side of the tires — the warmer the rubber, the more traction on the pavement, the tighter the turns.

What they're doing works, but the better and more efficient way is fast acceleration and hard braking.

After one go-around, we grid-up at the starter's line. There are four of us in the first row: me, number 36; Neil, number 22; ol' Mutton Chops Mike, a friend of ours, is number 4; and some dude I don't know who's decked out all in black is number 18. Mutton Chops gives Neil and me a friendly wave, lifts up his cutaway helmet so that his chin bar is up by his forehead, then wags his tongue at us, impersonating Gene Simmons. Neil greets him back with the sign of the devil. I smile and flip my tinted visor down. Neil, Mutton Chops, and Mr. Black follow my lead and we all turn to look straight ahead. This is my favourite part: getting your race head on, focusing, eye on the prize, the twitching inside that gets worse the longer you have to wait because you just want to peel the hell out of there.

The start marshal walks over to check if we're good to go. We are, and in my peripheral vision I watch him raise the flag over his head. I drop the clutch while revving the engine to the limit, but avoiding a wheelie. Dozens of riders behind us rev their machines. I can literally taste the anticipation — it's a combo of gas, rubber, tarmac, and a hint of Burt's chips.

The flag comes down hard and fast, and we become

this instant mass of screaming engines and smoking rubber as we haul ass down the track. We fly by pit road, and birds scatter in the far fields. Neil and Mike are in tight, flanking me hard, so I push it going into the first corner. I lean my bike over, my knee lightly kissing the ground as I glide through the turn. I'm the first coming out of it. Corners are my specialty. They're like breathing.

I barrel down the straightaway, counting four, five, six seconds in my head before downshifting into the tight left-hand hairpin. A quick check — Neil and Mutton Chops are glued at the hip with Mr. Black nipping at their heels. I come out of the bend and it's full throttle, reaching for that red line. As soon as the needle tips it, I pull back and drift over to my right, entering the series of S's. I give 'er hard as I come out of them, then gun it down the next straightaway because I know that's when Neil's going to try to make up time — a classic move my dad pointed out. He could read any rider like a book. *That guy keeps his arms and shoulders tense; that guy goes too fast into the corner, giving him bad under-steer.* And in Neil's case, *he brakes too late in the turns, loses time, and tries to make up for it in the straightaways, but then brakes late and brakes too hard.* Don't get me wrong, Neil's damn good. He also got an invite to the TT.

We fly by the grandstand, and I'm out front. I stay that way on the second and third lap, too. On the fourth,

I start working on a breakaway. I shoulder-check for encroachment. It so ain't happening. I've got a sweet lead now. Ha! Could put an eighteen-wheeler between me and Neil, and he said he was going to beat me. *I don't think so.* Count, four, five, six seconds, then downshift into the tight hairpin. No way he's gonna catch up. Man, I can't wait to see the look on Terry's face when I come into the pits — wait — *what?* Terry's not here. Concentrate. *Get back in the game.* I reach up to tear off a dirty strip from my visor and what happens next happens fast, because I blink and this scene appears behind my eyes. *Flash* I'm above myself looking down at me on the bike, but I'm not at Goodman's. *Flash* I'm back there, to that day, to that racetrack. I see Dad. He's out in front, ninth lap. I'm right behind him. Something falls from his bike — too quick to see it — his front wheel locks, there's black smoke before he's thrown over the handlebars and sent careening across the track … *Flash* instead of riding in the ambulance with him to the hospital, it's like I'm flying high above the paddock. The pits are empty and the race is over and everyone's gone home. Doris is the only vehicle in the lot, beside her a couple of lawn chairs and a cooler full of ice packs and beers. *Flash* I can see our T-shirts on our makeshift clothesline snapping in the wind. Then I wonder, *Who the hell packed up our stuff?* when I was pacing the hospital corridors and praying Dad would pull through. Who cleaned up our paddock? The track owners? No. Then it hits me. *Terry*. It had to have been. Who else? *Flash* I fly by the grandstand for my fifth lap.

I shoulder-check. Gap's closing. Why the frig am I thinking about this now? *Maybe 'cause you haven't talked to the guy — your dad's best friend — since the funeral. Terry, the guy who's practically family and now … and now, I don't know what the hell's going on.* The track in front of me starts to blur. I blink hard. Shit. I can't clear my eyes. Frig. I gotta get off the course. A part of me says no, but logic trumps ego. I thrust my arm out to warn the riders as I veer onto the runoff area. Neil and the others zip past me, and I catch Neil shoulder-checking to see if I'm okay.

I slow the bike to a stop and sit there feeling like a tool, trying to keep it together, trying to dry my eyes without wiping them so it's not obvious.

A corner marshal jogs across the grassy inner field toward me. "Son? Are you alright?" For a second — and I know this sounds stupid — I thought I'd heard my dad's voice. My heart's jackhammering like I've seen a ghost and I keep my visor down so the marshal can't see my face.

"You okay?" he repeats.

"Yeah," I say, doing my damnedest to steady my voice so he can't tell I'm lying, "I slipped the clutch too much off the start."

He nods, understanding.

Somehow I make it back to the paddock feeling like the world's biggest knob. I want to explode out of the place, but I can't because my race bike's not street legal. I wish I could climb into Doris and just take off, but that would mean ditching Mags and Neil.

I get my bike up onto its paddock stand, then lower Doris's tailgate to lie down in the box. I stare at the sky and listen to the race play-by-play on the overhead PA.

"Looks like this is going to be a close race with Scott Saunders out of the running. The three in front are Neil Bryant, 'Mutton Chops' Mike, and a surprise appearance from Jackson Adams, who's been fighting his way up from the back of the pack."

Huh, seems like Mr. Black, who was on the starter's grid with us is also having a bad race day. I hear the sound of someone jogging toward me. I sit up to see that it's Mags, looking concerned. I turn my head and make a fast wipe over my eyes and cheeks, hoping there are no track marks.

"Hey, Scott, you okay?"

"Yeah. I'm fine."

"What happened?"

"And Bryant's not leaving any room for error. But it looks like 'Mutton Chops' Mike is determined for a podium finish. Better watch it, Neil, this guy's fighting for the win."

"The clutch. It was slipping."

"Really?" Her green eyes dart right to the problem area. "Let me take a look at it —"

"Don't worry about it," but she's already going for her kit and pulling out tools. I jump down from the tail-gate and step between her and the machine. She stops, notices my block, and looks a little surprised. "Don't worry about it," I say as casually as I can, which isn't easy because there's a scratch in my voice.

She shrugs. "It's no problem."

I have to stare at the ground because I can't look at her with what I'm about to say next. "Mags. I want to be alone."

She starts backing away like I'm some kind of suicide jumper and slowly lowers her tools. Crap, I think. That came out all wrong.

"And it all comes down to this last turn … Neil makes a break for the inside, followed by Mutton Chops and Jackson. If Neil can maintain his lead, he's got this one all sewn up."

Spectators in the grandstand grow quiet; there's only the sizzle of fast food mixed with the distant whine of engines growing louder as they thunder toward the finish. I stand there, waiting to hear the inevitable as I watch Mags turn around and walk away.

"He's done it! It's Neil Bryant crossing the finish line, followed by a close second from Mutton Chops Mike and an impressive third from Jackson Adams. What a race this has been!"

chapter 4

Neil rides into the paddock and parks his bike next to mine. He flicks up his visor. "Hey, man, you okay? What happened?"

Well, I was thinking about my dad and I started bawling. I scrunch up my face, trying to mask my shame and embarrassment. "Clutch was slipping," I say, and this knot tightens in the pit of my stomach. We've known each other since we were six and I've never lied to him before.

He looks at me, then at my bike, then back at me again, and for a split second I wonder if he can tell I'm pulling one over on him.

"Ah, man. That's too bad," he says.

Neil doesn't rub his win in my face because he's a decent guy and a better friend than I deserve. He holds out his hand in a gesture of friendship and we do a half slap, half handshake.

Cathy comes running toward us, teetering on high heels, looking like a pit tootsie. She waves her hands. "You won! You won!" she cries and throws herself into Neil's arms. She can't kiss his face with the helmet on, so she settles for the visor, leaving a lipstick mark. Neil peels off the tearaway and holds it to his heart like it's a precious object. "I'll never throw this away," he says sarcastically and we all start laughing, including Cathy, who blushes.

Soon our racing buddies start dropping by. Mutton Chops Mike asks me — in a voice loud enough for the entire paddock to hear — what went wrong, and I find myself feeding him the same line. He nods like he understands and that gets him and the other guys trading stories about mechanical mishaps. I nod here and there to their tales of woe, but mostly keep my mouth clamped. I can feel my lie eating into my gut. I know Neil would have understood if I had told him, but now the timing's all wrong and I can't backpedal. It also doesn't help that I can see Mags scrutinizing my bike from afar like a bloodhound on a scent. I guess that's what makes mechanics, mechanics — their obsession with problem solving. If we didn't have them getting off on sticking their heads in greasy engine parts all day, we'd be screwed and bikes would blow apart on the track or something. I'll have to throw her off the scent somehow.

"So, I hear there's an after-party at Scott's place," Mutton Chops says.

"You got it," Cathy confirms, and before I know it, everyone's agreed to go. My smile is in danger of slipping, so I tuck my tight fists under my arms to keep it from unravelling. A house full of people is the last thing I want, but if I say no now, I'll look like a suck. All I want to do is take a shower, have a few beers, and put this day behind me.

Neil and Mutton Chops make their way back to the grandstand to bask in the podium glory, while I volunteer to tear down our pit and load up the bikes. Cathy said she'd give Neil a lift back, which means it's just Mags and me.

"Feel free to go with Cathy and Neil if you want," I tell her. "I can handle things here."

"No, I'll help," she says. "Unless you don't want me to."

I replay what I said to her earlier, how I'd needed some space. I cringe. I'm pretty sure that if she does have any hint of interest in me, I've probably squashed it. I let her pack up Neil's bike, but I make sure to handle my own.

We don't talk much on the ride home. What's there to say? *Sorry the first race of the season you saw me in I didn't finish? In fact, I choked? Can you believe I was actually invited to take part in the TT?* If only she could have seen me, Neil and my dad last year, climbing the leader-board. I bet she would have been impressed.

I back Doris into the driveway, park, and use my remote to open the garage doors.

Mags hauls her toolbox out of the truck and sets it down onto the workbench. She pulls a tool rag from her back pocket and tosses it over her shoulder.

"Want some help unloading?" she asks.

I look up at the machines sitting side by side like coin-operated kiddie rides outside the SafeMart. "I'm beat," I say. "Let's just leave them for now."

We head into the living room and the air feels stagnant and stuffy as hell. Dean's sprawled on the couch and his scuzzy friend Eddie is stretched out in my chair. The guy's like twenty-six years old. Why is he hanging around with Dean, who's eighteen? Something about Eddie bugs me. An empty bucket of Kentucky-fried pigeon and a poverty pack of cheap American beer sit on the floor. Both yahoos are insulting each other and yelling at the TV as they annihilate giant pandas with semi-automatics.

"Well, look at what the cat threw up — twice," I say. I pull back the curtains and jack open a window. The light that streams into the room makes the guys hiss like a pair of cockroaches.

I head upstairs to the bathroom, strip off my leathers, and stand under the shower nozzle for a total Hollywood shower, not caring how long I take or how much hot water I use. When the temperature grows cold, I shut off the taps and immediately feel a *thump-thump-thump* vibration of bass on my feet coming up through the bottom of the tub. Looks like the party's started. I dry off, change into a T-shirt and jeans, and head downstairs. The place is packed elbow to elbow.

In the living room people play video games or admire Dad's record collection. The kitchen is overrun by red plastic cups and Beer Pong teams. I glance out the back-door screen to see Neil, still in his leathers, hovering over the barbecue with a few of the guys. I see Mags too, standing by the bonfire alone. I grab a brew from the only part of the fridge no one bothers to pilfer from — the vegetable-crisper drawer.

"Better not touch my butterscotch pudding," a voice warns.

I laugh, shut the door, and see Dean. First thing I notice is the beer in his hand. "Where'd you get that?"

I ask. I've never seen the guy drink Creemore, let alone pay for one.

"Liberated it."

I snort. Yeah, right. Dean twists off the cap and flicks it between his thumb and middle finger so that it flies along the kitchen counter, ricochets off some girl's hand, and lands in the sink. "I hear Neil smoked your ass," he says. He starts thrusting his hips like he's giving it to me from behind. Dean looks so stupid and funny at the same time that it's impossible to get mad at him.

"Shut up, virgin," I say, and I can see by the look on his face that my cheap shot stings him, which means it must be true. *Oops*. I head outside before he can think of a comeback.

Mags is still by the bonfire. With the sun setting behind her and the fire in front of her, her red hair is all half light and half dark. She looks up and sees me and I hold up my beer in salutation. When she holds hers up, I see that she's drinking Creemore. Now I know who Dean "liberated" it from.

I'm about to head over to talk to her when Neil throws an arm over my shoulder. "Look, man," he says, pulling me toward the barbecue so he can flip over a nice-looking sirloin. "What happened to you today was unfortunate."

We watch the flames rise and lick the sizzling meat.

"Well, if you're really sorry, you can make me feel better by giving me your steak," I say.

Neil shakes his head apologetically. "My feelings don't run *that* deep."

We chuckle and from somewhere in the house, I think Neil's room, comes the sound of Cathy laughing, hysterically. I think everyone in the entire yard can hear her.

Neil and I look back at his dinner and inhale the scent of cooked meat. I'm about to tell him what really went on today, because I know he'd understand why I lied. Neil was there for me when my dad died, big time, and it's something I won't forget.

Mutton Chops comes over and offers his hand to Neil.

"Good race, man," he says, shaking Neil's hand, then Mutton Chops looks at me, shakes his head, and scratches at one of his chops like he's digging for oil. "I can't believe I beat ol' Scotty Saunders. Lord Almighty, it's a miracle. One for the record books, eh?"

"Yeah, yeah," I say and to show I'm a good sport, I bow before him. Neil and Mutton Chops laugh, and I take my leave to more important matters over by the bonfire.

Great. While I've been goofing around, greasy Eddie's moved in. He's standing really close to Mags, like they're friends or something.

"So," he's says, pulling one of her curls straight, "when are you going to let me take you out?"

She knocks his hand away, and the closer I get, the more I can smell the beer on him. It's bad enough I have to put up with Dean, but his scuzz-ball friend hitting on Mags is more than I can take. I get right into his face. "The answer is never, so back off."

His nostrils flare. "Why don't you get lost?" he says.

"Yeah? Why don't you get off my property?"

He steps back and puts his hands up, making like he's all innocent, but he looks more like a perp on the TV show *Cops*. "Hey, man. We're just talking. What, are you her boyfriend or something?"

I want to shove him, maybe even take a swing, but if I do that, she'll know how I feel. Screw it. I shove him anyway.

He stumbles back a few steps, then charges me. He's so drunk I barely need to side-step to make sure he doesn't end up in the fire. I wait for him to turn around so he can see what's coming next — my fist — but then Neil gets between us. "Guys, guys, guys," he says, doing his Jesus pose. "Come on. Be cool."

I dismiss Eddie with a quick nod to show that he's not worth it, and when I turn to see if Mags is okay, she's gone. I look around but can't see her in the crowd. I head back inside the house and the Beer Pong crowd piles out from the kitchen, blocking my way. Friggin' Eddie.

I check the kitchen, the living room, then go upstairs to knock on her door, but there's no answer. I break out in a sweat. Shit. She must know that I like her and she's taken off because the feeling isn't mutual and she doesn't want to face me. She probably feels embarrassed for me.

When I come back downstairs again, I see a thin strip of light at the bottom of the door leading to the garage.

Oh crap.

I turn the knob and let the door drift open. There's Mags up on the box, flashlight in hand, and getting in real close to my bike.

My heart goes from pumping to thumping.

She looks over, sees me, then stands up. Best to come clean, I think. You can't lie to a mechanic. The proof's always right in front of them.

"I didn't slip the clutch, I choked." I say it fast, like ripping off a bandage.

"I knew it wasn't my work." She jumps down from Doris and tucks her flashlight into her back pocket. "No worries, your secret's safe with me." She picks up her beer to show me that it's empty. "You want one?" she asks.

"Sure," I say and think, *That's it?* No asking why I lied? "Don't you want to know why?" I ask.

She shakes her head. "Not really. We all have our off days. If you'd wanted to tell me, you would've."

Her laid-back attitude suddenly makes me want to spill the truth.

I'm about to open my mouth when a white oversize van backs into the driveway. Written on the rear windows in cursive letters are the words *Terry's Cycle*. This catches me off-guard. What the heck is Terry doing here? Then I remember Neil saying that he was getting his new race bike tonight. Terry cuts the van's engine, gets out, then shuts the driver's door. I see he hasn't changed much: goatee, black T-shirt and jeans, and thirty-year-old biker boots. I don't know why I was expecting something different.

"Hey, Terry," I say and my voice sounds flat.

I guess he picks up on it because he can barely look me in the eye. "Hey, Scott." Then his lips tighten as if the half-smile he's sporting causes him pain. He nods to Mags.

"I'll go get Neil," Mags says, and before I know it, she's heading around the side yard to the back of the house. Now it's just Terry, me, and a long stretch of silence.

"You get out to Goodman's today?" he asks.

I fight to keep the image of him cleaning up our paddock out of my mind. I never thanked him for what he did. "Yeah."

He nods. "Good. You'll want to get in all the track time you can. You'll be great at the TT." His eyes wander past my shoulder and at something a million miles away, and I see that pained smile again. If he's trying to twist up my guts with a torque wrench, he's doing a terrific job. There was a time when he had wanted to go to the TT just as badly as I did, and now it's like I don't exist, like we're strangers now. I dunno. Am I missing something? Is he mad that I still want to go through with the race? Is this why he's been avoiding me?

Mags returns with Neil, Cathy, Mutton Chops, and about a dozen others in tow.

"Terry!" Neil cries and shakes his hand. Terry pops open the van's back doors and hops in. He slides the loading ramp out for Neil, who takes it from him, then gets passed a new paddock stand. Someone whistles sarcastically at the stand, like it's a thing of beauty, making us laugh. A second later Terry rolls the machine down the ramp and into the light. It's a beautiful CBR600RR in neon green, Neil's favourite colour, and barely off the factory floor. He hands it over to Neil, who sets it on its new paddock stand. We all inhale that factory-fresh smell. It's heaven.

"Sweet Mother of God, what a ride," Dean says.

I look over at Neil. His eyes are stupidly big and go along perfectly with his wide-open gob. I know he's dying to reach out and caress the bike's pristine fairing, aching to hoist his leg up over the seat and slide down onto the vinyl groove and imagine himself twisting the throttle and flying. I know, because I've been there.

Everyone crowds around his new toy like kids muscling in to see a rare hockey card. Neil's on her now. He puffs out his chest, places his feet on the pegs, and is about to lean forward and grip the throttle.

"What a beauty, eh?" someone says.

There's a rapid-fire exchange of approving looks between everyone except the happy couple. Cathy's crossed arms and unblinking eyes charge the air with a different kind of energy, one with a hint of a storm.

Of course, Dean starts snickering. The guy bathes in conflict.

Cathy says the words "How much?" to Neil and we're all ears.

"You knew I was going to buy it."

For the first time, the girl who never stops talking is speechless. Neil swings a leg over the CBR and we break our circle so the two of them can pass and continue talking on the front lawn. Phrases like "you know, our future plans" and "down payment" skip across the patches of new grass.

Mags produces a flashlight from her back pocket and crouches, getting close to the CBR's engine. "To get it ready we'll need to install a steering damper, upgrade the front and rear shocks, rearsets, replace the bodywork, stainless-steel brake lines ..." She gets down on the floor so she can better aim the flashlight in behind the fairing. Everyone's watching her. "... change the gearing, black box, ignition remapped, and then she'll be ready for the heavy work."

"Better stop, Mags," Dean warns. "I think Eddie here's about to cream his j—"

"What kind of tires are you going to use?" I blurt out. I already know, but I want to stop the ass from humiliating her. Then I shoot Eddie a "Don't get any ideas and shut your cake-hole while you're at it" look.

"Dunlop," Neil pipes in, squeezing Cathy's hand as they join us again.

"Pirelli," Mags corrects him.

Neil turns to Terry. "A spot is always open if you change your mind and want to go with us."

Terry glances at me, then looks away fast, and that

awkward thing comes back again. "Well," he says, "I don't mind ordering your parts wholesale and having Maggie use my shop, but that's the best I can do." He walks over to Neil's old race bike and gets ready to haul it away in the van.

Dean shoves his hands into his pockets. "Neil, you sure you want Mags prepping your race bike? She's barely out of diapers."

This time it's Terry who jumps to her defence. "Don't talk about my best mechanic like that. She knows what she's doing."

Mags's cheeks turn red.

"Huh, wrench-wench," Dean says.

Cathy swats him on the arm, hard. "God, shut up. You're so annoying."

Mags hauls herself up off the floor and high-fives Cathy.

chapter 5

"Jesus H. Murphy, that's a lot of turns."

Good ol' Dean, telling it like it is. He sits in the living room, strumming his guitar, staring at a map of the TT course on the coffee table.

The course, thirty-seven and three-quarter miles, has more than two hundred bends.

Mags has been quizzing me and Neil every morning and night on each of the mile markers. She's been great. We keep inviting her to come with us, but she changes the subject. She's one mysterious girl. I think I'm in love. After putting in a full day's work at the garage she comes home and continues stripping Neil's new bike, doing most of the bulk. Vince and Marco keep putting Neil off, saying that their paid gigs are more important right now than doing free work. It's making me edgy, but if Neil says things will be okay, I know him well enough to trust that things will be.

"Name the obstacle at Bungalow," Mags says before taking a sip of her tea.

"Train tracks, or 'tram tracks,'" I say.

"Good. Did you guys see that video I bookmarked and sent you yesterday?"

"Yeah, I've watched it like forty times already. It's a good one." It's an old onboard lap with Nick Jefferies, who narrates in detail. "Thanks for finding it."

"No problem. Now, which of the twelve sectors will you take the fastest all the way through?"

It's Neil's turn to answer. "Sector two. It's almost flat out from the start at Union Mills through to Greeba Castle."

"How many klicks from the start is it to Ginger Hall hotel?"

"Just under thirty-three," I answer.

"Milestone twenty-six, name it."

"Joey's," Neil says.

"Gooseneck," Mags supplies. "Does it come before or after the waterworks?"

"After," we both answer.

Dean slurps up his bowl of pale pink cereal milk. "Did you know that the Bee Gees were born on the Isle of Man?"

We all stop to look at him, surprised.

"Yeah, it's true." He starts drumming on his guitar and sings the opening bars to "Stayin' Alive" in falsetto.

Of all the records from my dad's collection Dean chose to listen to, I never would have guessed the Bee Gees. I wonder if somebody's been slipping something into his Apple Jacks.

An hour later at work, the gunmetal-grey door to Russ's office swings open and smacks against the concrete wall, making everyone on the cannery floor look up. Dean storms out and rejoins me on the line. Today's catch: salmon.

"What's up?" I ask.

"Asked the bossman for an extra shift and you know what that asshole said? 'I don't think so.'"

Other line workers sneak glances at us, well, mostly at Dean when they think he's not looking. They're probably wondering if he's the one behind all the thefts around here. Not only are lockers getting broken into, but now cars are, too, and since everyone in this town knows he spent time in juvie for breaking and entering, it doesn't take a genius to connect the dots. I try to think of something Neil would say to lighten the mood, because I don't want to work next to a guy who's upset and wielding a knife.

"Frig, man. You and me, we'll be cashing our fishery pension cheques in this crap-shack town." Wait, what did I just say? That's not helpful at all. Man, if the guy goes postal, it'll be my fault.

He scoffs. "Yeah, right. You can leave this dive any-time you want."

"Yeah, well, so can you."

Not taking his eyes off his work, he shakes his head and says in a serious tone, "No. No, I can't, Scott. People don't whisper 'thief' when they see you coming." He picks up another fish, slaps it down, then slices off its head with one swift chop. "I got no place to go but down."

I'm not sure what to say. It grows quiet on the line, just the sounds of the belt moving and knives cutting through meat. Dean bites his lower lip. It looks like he's trying hard to keep his anger in check.

"What I don't get is why you're working here," he says. "You don't need the money. I know you own your house outright."

I'm surprised he knows that. I guess Neil told him, or he figured it out. He's right, I do live mortgage-free.

"So how come you're not in college like Neil?"

I'm about to tell him the same answer I'd been using to get people off my back, that my grades were shit, but it's not true. In fact, I had been accepted to the University of British Columbia last fall. "After my dad died, I just didn't feel like going to school."

He keeps his head down. "Sorry, man."

"Yeah, well. What can you do other than kill time at Ferber's until the TT? My dad, Terry, Neil, and I were planning the trip for a long time." I'm surprised at how easy all this is falling out of my mouth. I grab another salmon and wonder why I'm opening up to this guy, of all people. I clam up and change the subject. "So if you hate this place so much, how come you're asking for more shifts?"

I have to clean three more fish before I get an answer.

"Neil invited me to go to the TT."

I set down my knife. It's hard to gut fish when you feel like you've just been gutted yourself. I feel like Neil's turning this trip into a joke. He's got cousins who don't seem to give a damn, and now he's brought Dean on board without checking with me first? "When did he ask you to go?"

Two short blasts over the PA signal break time, and Dean stabs the knife into the cutting board, making it stand upright. "Who cares, I ain't going, am I? Russ won't give me the time of day. I'm sure the asshole would love to fire me."

He tears off his apron and hairnet and walks away. I stand there, my mind flooded with a million thoughts. How does Neil invite Dean without checking with me first? He knows I think the guy's a dick.

I remove my gloves and untie my apron. Secretly I'm glad Dean's screwed himself and that he's got no chance of going.

Everyone on the floor hears Dean kick the wall outside the locker room.

Hours later, when it's quitting time, I line up with the others to clock out, and Russ comes over, pulling me aside. He tells me that there's an extra shift if I want it.

I can't even stand to look at the guy when I say no. It should have been Dean's shift.

I come home after work and immediately change into my sweats. I'm going to work Neil out so hard he's not going to know what hit him.

He gets changed and meets me in the backyard. The ground's a soggy mess from the spring thaw, but it's nothing we can't handle. Flipping tractor tires is an old-school workout, like swinging kettle bells, but it's ten times better than anything you can do in a gym. We break out in a sweat in no time and soon our clothes are caked in mud.

I grunt and push the tire over. It lands in the mud with a *splat*. "So when were you going to tell me that you invited Dean?"

Neil grits his teeth as he hoists his tire off the ground. "Yeah, sorry, man, I meant to tell you yesterday."

I cock one eyebrow at him, calling him on his bullshit.

"Okay, okay. I knew you'd say no."

"You're damn straight. What were you going to have him do? Be in charge of the fuel? I can just see it, Dean in the pits, refilling our tanks with a smoke hanging from his lips. Kaboom."

Neil's tire drops to the ground. "Why do you hate the guy so much?"

"I think the question is why do you *like* the guy so much?"

He wipes the sweat from his brow with the back of his forearm. "Look, we both know I don't have a chance in hell of making it through qualifying week at the TT, so it'd be nice to have some fun."

My jaw drops. Did I just hear him say that?

"You've got what it takes," he continues, "but I don't,

not really. So why can't we just have a good time and come back with some great memories?"

"What the hell are you talking about? You'll qualify."

This time he cocks his eyebrow at me. "You think I'm going to come in at 115 percent of the third-fastest rider's lap time in order to qualify? Just because you get an invite, doesn't mean you make it to race day. I don't have the course down like you do, Scott. And corners are your thing, not mine."

"So we practice," I say. I add a tone to my voice that says, *Stop with the self-loathing*. "Now pick up the god-damn tire!" I bark, so that it sounds half funny and half like I don't want to discuss this anymore.

We get back to flipping again. Only now when I pick up my tire, it feels a million pounds heavier. His lack of confidence unnerves me. Maybe Cathy's getting to him.

Weeks pass. If we thought we'd been studying the course before, it's nothing compared to now. I make us memorize the twenty-six course markers and which of the four quadrants they're in. We've also banned ourselves from watching TT crash videos on-line. That's all we need rolling through our skulls when we get there.

Vincent and Marco actually make an appearance and we start solidifying plans. We take Terry up on his offer to purchase parts wholesale and use his shop to finish working on Neil's race bike, although I let those guys head up that part of things. If Terry doesn't want to see me, then I don't want to see him. It's just better that way. I work on my race bike in the garage, getting it crated up to be shipped overseas.

On Sunday, Neil and I switch up our workouts from jogging and tire flipping to mountain biking. Today we're hitting the Devil Bear, an intense bike trail on Mount Kinnen, known to deliver a hefty helping of "whup ass." It's not for the Sunday rider either. There are some sixty-degree-angle climbs, chutes, ladders, bridges, log jumps, steep switchbacks, and in some places, six- to ten-metre drops. Your tires don't spend much time on the ground and your front shocks get quite a beating.

Three hours later, dog-tired and sweaty, we pedal for home. I don't know about Neil, but I'm ready to drop. We turn off the road into the driveway, and the first thing we see is Cathy's VW bug. She gets out of the car and slams the door hard enough to make the vehicle shake. She's dressed up, even more than usual, like it's church service or something, and I realize I've never seen her look this upset, let alone mad.

Before Neil can park his bicycle and wipe the sweat from his brow, Cathy's marched over to him and stands there with hands on hips.

"Please don't tell me you forgot about coming to my parents' place for lunch to meet my grandmother."

His eyes grow big, then squeeze shut as he winces. Cathy gasps. "I called you, like, twenty times."

Neil looks to his bike pouch where he keeps his phone. "Sorry. I guess I didn't hear it." Dean comes strolling out of the house with his guitar and a cigarette in his mouth. He parks his butt on the front stoop, lights his smoke, and starts strumming.

Cathy folds her arms. "You said Sundays were your day off."

Neil looks at me, then at the ground, like a kid who's been caught.

"It's totally my fault," I add. "I talked him into it."

In Neil's defence, he does look sorry. He holds his hands out to the sides, palms facing out. "Give me fifteen minutes," he says. "I'll shower and change. I'll make it up to you and your grand —"

Cathy stares at his Jesus pose, steps back, and says in a calm voice, "Oh, no no no. You can't charm your way out of this. Do you know how embarrassed I was when you didn't show up? All I did was talk you up to Grandma.

My dad even refelted the pool table and my mom made her blueberry cheesecake."

"Damn," he says, "I love her blueberry cheesecake."

Wow. That sounded lame, even coming from him.

"I hardly see you in weeks because you're either working or training, and when we do get together on your only day off, you either bail on me or all you want to do is sleep."

Dean snorts.

"Shut up, Dean!" she snaps, then her eyes grow suddenly glassy. "You spend more time with your motorcycle than me." She crosses her arms over her chest and bites her lip. I realize the more she's upset, the calmer her voice.

"I'm sorry I don't know how to ride," she goes on. "I'm sorry I don't even like being on a bike. I'm sorry I'm not into it like Mags." I raise my eyebrows. Is Cathy jealous of Mags? Then Cathy starts sobbing and before we know it, she's walking away, hugging herself.

"Cathy, wait," Neil pleads.

She heads for her car, and Neil follows.

Dean pinches the heater off the tip of his smoke and tucks the unused portion back into his pack. He and I both head inside.

In the living room we can still hear them talking.

"... but you knew this is what I liked to do when you met me."

"I know, but ..."

Dean strums his guitar and sings, "'... American woman / she gonna mess your mind ...'"

I stare at the TT wall, taking in some stats — like how the top of Snaefell Mountain is 620 metres above sea level.

Dean strums a few more bars, then puts his guitar down and heads into the kitchen.

"What a bitch," he says and opens the fridge. I just know he's going for one of my beers in the vegetable-crisper drawer. "Neil needs to dump her ass."

"Hey, don't call her a bitch," I say, but he's already heading up the stairs, twisting off the beer top, and shutting his bedroom door. "And keep your hands off my beer," I add. "Friggin' mooch."

I hear a car door slam, then an engine start. Out the front window I see Cathy's VW take off down the road. I grab a shower and stuff my face with leftover chicken from yesterday's barbecue.

The kitchen phone rings and I answer it. It's Mags, and she's calling from work.

"Hey, Scott. Is Neil there? He's not answering his phone and we're supposed to be heading out to

Goodman's for Track Day to test drive his bike."

The phone cord stretches just long enough for me to open the garage door, and I see Neil on his bike turning down the drive, likely following Cathy. I update Mags on the fight they just had.

"Damn," she says. "We've got track time booked and everything. I need to see how the bike handles before I have to take it apart and ship it out."

Now she's taking it apart and shipping it for him? I hope Neil's throwing a few bucks her way. She's not even going with us.

"Where are Vince and Marco?"

"They headed back to Vancouver an hour ago."

"Oh," I say. I don't like how any of this is going down. Neil and I need to have a serious talk. "Why don't I pop by with the truck and we can load up the bike?" I say.

"That'd be great, Scott."

It occurs to me that Neil never asked to use my truck to transport his bike to Goodman's. I mean, it's no big deal, but forgetting that, along with his date to meet Cathy's grandmother? Something's going on.

I head out to Terry's Cycle. Terry's van isn't there and I'm kinda relieved. I just want to load up and get out. When we're finished securing Neil's race bike onto the truck, I try calling Neil again. This time he answers.

"Hey, man, Mags is ready to test out your bike. Where are you?"

"I'm over at Cathy's. I can't talk and I can't leave right now."

"He's at Cathy's and he says he can't leave," I relay to Mags.

She pulls a notebook from her locker. "Tell him he has to," she replies.

"Neil, it's your only shot before we head out. You don't want to be breaking the bike in on the TT course."

He sighs, obviously frustrated. "Frig, I can't. Things are critical here. If I leave now it could be over between us. She wants me to quit racing or quit her."

Somehow I knew that conversation was coming. I exhale a deep breath. "Oh boy."

"Hey, do me a favour? Go with Mags and ride it for me."

"What? Are you serious?"

"Yeah. Do what you need to do. I trust your instincts."

I feel a thrill shoot up from my gut and spread across my chest. I knew a spare gear kit and leathers in the back of the truck would come in handy one day. Then I hesitate. "But it's your new toy. You sure?"

I hear Cathy in the background. "Neil?"

"Yeah. I'm positive. I gotta go. I'll try and meet up with you if I can. Thanks, man." He hangs up.

Mags comes over to me. "What'd he say?"

"He wants me to do it for him."

"Okay," she says, "let's go."

On the way to Goodman's, we talk about racing conditions and how to best calibrate the bike because it'll have to climb more than two thousand feet above sea level.

Mags leans toward the dashboard to get a better look at the dark clouds gathering over the mountains. She points to them. "Don't you dare rain," she says in a half-threatening tone.

"I figure we've got an hour if we're lucky."

We arrive at Goodman's. People are packing up for the day, which is good because it means fewer bikes on the track. I park in the pre-grid area, where we unload and I suit up. All we need is enough time for Mags to make some notes to give to Vince and Marco and get the engine smoothed out. I warm up his bike, revving the engine. A twinge of guilt hits me because it should be Neil doing this, but I let the feeling go and concentrate on doing the best job I can for him.

"Okay, Scott. Go up to five thousand rpm's and then work it up to ten. I want to check things over before you take it up to the red line."

Mags steps back and I head down the track.

I take it easy, shifting between gears smoothly and

easily. The engine sounds great. So far, Mags has done an incredible job. I'm not anywhere near four thousand rpm's and already I can tell it's a sweet ride.

When the tires start grabbing traction, I take 'er up to seven thousand. So smooth and easy. I return to Mags after the first lap.

"So, how's it handling?" she asks.

"Pretty good. I'm thinking more rebound on the front to keep it planted better, but on the first time out, it feels like a racer. Good job."

She ignores my compliment. Her face is one-hundred percent business as she adjusts the forks. I head off for a half-dozen laps and report back again. On the third go-around I take it up to the red line and start gliding in and out of the corners. It's like sailing and flying at the same time. Man, what I could do with this bike would be phenomenal. I'm seriously jealous.

I slow to a stop in front of Mags and remove my helmet. I'd like to take 'er for another lap, but it's like someone's drawn a heavy curtain over the sky.

"You," I say to Mags, "would give any seasoned race mechanic a run for his money."

This time my comment hits the jackpot. She lowers her head to hide her smile, but I can still see it.

Lightning arcs across the sky from east to west.

"Wow, did you see that?" Mags points, then rests her hand on my shoulder. I don't move. My flesh tingles under my leathers.

We watch the light show for a few minutes, but I can hardly take it in. Having her this close makes me feel drunk. A blast of cold wind hits us, tossing her hair around, and I smell her shampoo: vanilla and oranges.

Mags lifts her hand off my shoulder and I guess the moment we had was all in my head. I lightly pat the gas tank.

"She's a real beaut," I say. I look at Mags and I feel the heat rise in my face because it sounded like I was saying that about her. I wasn't, but hell, it fits. Mags gives me this amazing smile and I feel like ... like she's just jacked me with nitrous oxide, and before I can think about what to say or do next, it's like time's slowed down. Mags reaches out and gently places her hand on the back of my neck and pulls me toward her as she leans in for a kiss. *No way!* My lips touch hers, and all I can think is that I can't believe I'm kissing her. I'm kissing Mags. I set my helmet down so I can tear off my gloves to hold her face in my hands as I pull her closer. It still feels like I'm on the bike, flying. I never want this moment to end.

Hail the size of marbles forces us apart as it rains down hard and bounces across the tarmac. We half laugh, half cry out from pain, and Mags steals my helmet and thrusts it on her head as we hustle like crazy to get the bike loaded and a tarp thrown over it. Lightning splits the sky again and the thunder cracks almost immediately. By the time we hop into the truck, bike safely stowed, we're soaked, but having a good laugh about it. I fire up Doris, switch on the defrost and crank the heater to high.

"Wow, it's really coming down," Mags says, rubbing her hands together.

I reposition the dashboard vents so the heat blows her way, then I dare to put my arm around her and draw her in close so she can warm up faster. She shivers against my chest and our lips find each other as we start kissing again. More flying.

Hail pummels the cab. It's my new favourite sound, next to her laughter. She slowly pulls away, kisses each of my eyelids, and I curl a lock of hair behind her ear.

"I wondered when we were finally going to kiss," she says.

I smile. "I didn't know you wanted me to."

She sits up a little. "Are you kidding me? I only gave you a million signs."

"What?" I say, surprised. "What signs?"

She puts a finger on my lips to shush me and we make out until the hail turns into a steady downpour of rain. When my stomach grumbles, loudly, we decide it's time to head back to change out of our wet clothes and grab a bite. I'm hoping the house is empty so we have it to ourselves. I turn on the windshield wipers and switch on my headlights.

The blades snap back and forth and can barely keep up with the rain. I slide my arm around Mags's shoulders, and she slips out of her shoulder belt so she can snuggle next to me, resting her head on my chest. She fits perfectly.

We're about a quarter of the way home, on Highway 7A, when I see two vehicles up ahead. One of them is a 4x4 truck and the other is an old tank of a car with its hood propped up. They've stopped in the middle of the road, but it's all wrong-looking. There's a bumper lying on the ground, along with shattered pieces of a tail light.

"I think the truck just rear-ended that car," I say and switch on my hazards before pulling over. "Call 9-1-1," I tell her and get out of the truck. Within seconds I'm drenched in cold rain.

I jog over to the truck. It must have just happened because the driver, a teenager barely big enough to see over the dashboard, is still staring ahead in shock.

I rap my knuckles on the window. "Hey, you okay?" I shout loud enough so he can hear me.

The kid jumps a little, like I've snapped him out of

a trance. He nods, so I jog over to the other vehicle and see an old lady. She's got both hands on the wheel at ten and two o'clock.

I knock on her window. "Ma'am? Are you alright?"

When she turns to look at me, I see blood pouring from her nose and her yellow spring jacket is covered in it. My guess is that she hit the steering wheel. I tell her I'm going to open the door and she nods.

"Are you alright?" I ask again.

She manages to say yes, then points a shaky finger in front of her. "My car wouldn't start. There was a young man helping me."

I can't see jack where she points because she's got the hood up, so I jog around to the front of the vehicle.

What I see next rips the breath out of me. There, parked by the shoulder, highlighted by her car's headlights, is a black-and-silver motorcycle.

Neil's bike.

I scan the road, the shoulder, and the ditch. "Neil!" I yell. I can't see or hear a damn thing in this rain.

"Neil!"

Of course, it has to be him. Who else would stop to help a little old lady with car troubles?

I locate his helmet a few metres away. Where *is* he? I look back and study the angle of the woman's car. If she was hit when Neil was looking under the hood, then that means … I jog across to the other side of the road and along the gravel shoulder. The rainwater runs down the bank, joining the muddy torrent flowing in the ditch. I take one more step and that's when I see him, in the ditch, the lower two-thirds of his body underwater.

I sink down on my knees next to him. "Neil?"

He opens his eyes. "Scott?" he manages to say. "I got hit."

His teeth are dark — I think it's his blood.

"I was helping this lady with her car." He coughs and blood runs down his cheek, mixing with the rain.

"She got rear-ended by a truck. Mags has called 9-1-1. Help will be here any minute." I unzip my jacket and fan it out behind me like a cape, then bend forward over his face, acting as a shield from the rain. What first-aid I remember comes back to me. *You don't let them sleep.*

Neil closes his eyes.

"Hey. Don't close your eyes. Keep them open, man. Talk to me."

His mouth opens and closes like he's taking guppy breaths. "Tell Cathy I'm sorry about everything," he says.

I immediately hate what he's saying because it sounds all final and shit. I shake my head. "No way. You want her to know that, *you* tell her."

About a quarter mile down the road, I can see blue-and-white flashing lights. "Ambulance is coming." I stand up and wave my arms. Mags sees me and comes running over.

When she sees Neil, she slaps a hand over her mouth. "Oh my god."

I crouch down again and try to protect him as best as I can. "Hang on, buddy."

He closes his eyes and when I nudge him, he doesn't open them. I do it again, only harder.

The ambulance pulls to a stop and a paramedic gets out, slams the door, and comes running over.

"You see what happened?" one of them asks me.

I can barely see his face with the lights flashing behind him. "My friend was fixing that lady's car and they got rear-ended by the truck."

Another paramedic comes running over and I move to the side so he can check Neil's pulse. "No vitals," he says to his partner. "You're going to need to stand back," he tells us.

"Oh my god," Mags whispers.

I take a step back and watch them work on my best friend as he lies there in a ditch … dying.

And my world tilts again.

chapter 6

Neil died from massive internal injuries on the way to the hospital.

We haven't left the house in days. The place feels empty without him. Dean's been parked in the living room chain-smoking and going through my dad's records. He plays Joni Mitchell's "Blue" album over and over. Joni's melancholy voice fills the place with the words we don't know how to say ourselves. Mags sits in the kitchen pushing toast around her plate, and I'm in the upstairs bathroom staring down at a twisted tube of toothpaste. In my mind I hear echoes of Neil's voice asking why no one seems to know how to use the toothpaste like a normal human being. "It's not that hard, guys," he'd shout at us from behind the door. "All you have to do is roll it up from the bottom." And we'd crack up because one of us had squashed and twisted it out of shape on purpose, just to bug him.

I reach down and flatten the tube smooth.

I feel numb all of the time and whenever I think I can do something simple like get out of bed or breathe, my mind relives what happened and I get this painful punch-to-the-gut feeling. I don't know if I'm coming or going, so I just wander from room to room, and for some reason I find myself putting things away. Trying to make some order, I guess.

I dunno.

At two-thirty we gather in the living room, all of us dressed in black for his funeral. I've loaned Dean one of my dad's ties and he's got it around his neck, but he stares at the two ends of it like it's a cruel joke. He slumps and closes his raw, salmon-pink-coloured eyes. Mags steps forward and with a gentle touch she knots the tie for him.

On the way to the funeral service, Mags sits between Dean and me. There's a gap between her leg and mine that might as well be the width of a canyon. We haven't touched since we kissed that day. It's like it never happened. It doesn't feel right to mention it either.

We drive down the highway for the next twenty minutes in silence, passing endless acres of empty, mud-soaked fields.

"If it hadn't been for that bitch," Dean says, using a sledgehammer to break the stillness, "he never would have been out in the rain."

I keep quiet. What am I going to say that'll make it better? Nothing. Cathy didn't have anything to do with it. It was an accident, that's all. Dean mumbles something else, but I can't hear him. He's got his forehead pressed against the passenger-side window.

We come up over the crest of Purple Hill and see dozens of vehicles waiting to pull into the church. Those already in the parking lot snake around slowly, trying to find a place to park. By the time we arrive, one of several ushers has come out of the church and is directing people to park on the grass. We do, and all three of us get out of the truck. For all the people in the lot, it's strangely quiet except for the slow-moving cars, doors opening and closing, and the crunch of gravel underfoot.

I reach for the wrought-iron door handle and pull it open. Dark-sounding organ music spills out.

I hate this.

My dad's funeral was here. Guys from all over the country, the United States, and Europe came to pay their respects. At the reception afterwards, one of the top racers said to me that he thought it was the way my dad would have wanted to go — riding out to the very end — and I remembered thinking no, it wasn't. We were supposed to go up north camping after the race and, on our way, take a detour to the University to pick up a course book so I could get his take on some fall classes. The guy wanted to live the next forty or fifty years.

People crowd the back of the church and stand with their coats unbuttoned or draped over their arms. It smells like sweat and flowers in here and everyone's talking in hushed voices. Mags, Dean, and I leave our jackets on and say nothing.

A tall, thin man in a dark suit with hands clasped like he's praying comes over and tells us that the service is about to begin and that he's afraid there's no more seating and that we'll have to stand. We position ourselves behind the back of the last pew. There must be more than 250 people in here already with more still coming in. I knew Neil had lots of friends, but I had no idea he had this many. I recognize about three-dozen faces from biking. The rest must be relatives, Cathy and her family, people he met at college, and his co-workers from his job at the Community Rec Centre where he worked part-time.

When I look over the heads of the people seated in the pews and at the altar up front, my mouth goes dry. Inside that closed maple box with a spray of white flowers draped over it is Neil. He's gone and it sucks and it's not right.

Dean stares at his shoes, the ceiling, the stained-glass windows, and I realize he's just working his way up to the front. Mags chews her bottom lip and I can tell she's fighting back tears. I wish I was the touchy-feely type. I think about what Neil would do and take a step closer so we make a tight half-circle.

A woman starts sobbing and the sound echoes throughout the space, over the organ music. It's the deep, heavy kind of crying that can bring a man to his knees because there's nothing he can do to fix it. It hurts to see that it's coming from Cathy. She sits next to Neil's parents with her face buried in tissues. What's left of my busted-up heart crumbles. No matter what I thought of her voice and cheerleader pep, she made my buddy's face light up. I shake my head. None of this is right. They should have moved in together, gotten married, bought a house, had kids. I want to go up there and tell her how sorry I am, and I will, but the timing's off. I know Neil's folks don't want to see me right now. They had been okay with me until Neil decided he wanted in on the TT trip and joined my dad, Terry, and me when we went road racing in Ireland in order to qualify. His folks had constantly been on his case about retiring from racing.

They had wanted him to concentrate on becoming a kinesiologist. So Neil had moved out and that's when the Saunders name was banned in his household.

They'd gotten Neil all wrong, though. After my dad died (I'm sure Neil's folks came down twice as hard on him when they found out the death was racing-related), Neil was the one who helped me get my life back together. He got me out of the house, stopped me from drinking and sleeping all day, and made me submit my TT application before the deadline. He even tried to get Terry and me together, only that part didn't quite work out. Somehow it was okay for his cousins to work on cars and partake in some rally races, but it wasn't okay for Neil to ride a motorcycle.

Cathy dabs her eyes with the tissues and straightens up in her seat a little, doing a good job of composing herself. She glances over her shoulder and at the crowd as if she too can't believe the turnout. When her eyes catch mine I press my lips together in an attempt to say, "Sorry," and "I miss him too," and a million other feelings they don't have words for, but I can't tell if she got any of it. Her expression's blank.

The organ stops playing and, for a few seconds, notes still hang in the air. The minister appears and starts telling us that our beloved Neil died too young and that our loss is the beginning of his life ever after.

I can't say I'm much of a religious guy, but I do recognize some passages he reads, like the one about the Lord being my shepherd and walking through the valley of the shadow of death and fearing no evil. I think Neil would have liked that fearing-no-evil part, because he didn't. Then Neil's uncle gets up and says a few words about his star nephew, how everyone liked him, the great man he would have become, and the role model he'd already been. After him, our old high-school teacher, Coach Turner, talks about Neil's good grades and his athletic accomplishments. When he mentions Neil's work with kids at the pool and how he volunteered to teach at-risk youth to swim on his own time, off the clock, Dean's bottom lip quivers a little. That's how Neil and Dean met. He was one of those at-risk kids. Tears spill down Dean's face and he doesn't try to cover them up by scratching his cheek or anything. I never thought Dean would show his vulnerable side like this in public, or to anyone. I guess Neil was the only one who got through to him.

No one up there mentions my buddy's love for bikes. It's like they all agreed to shove that part of him away, as if it were the motorcycle that did him in. What no one knew is that Neil was never more himself than when he was on a bike. He always said that riding was nirvana, that it connected him to something bigger. People here would have known that if someone had asked one of us to speak. I would have done it.

Some music plays, a country song that none of us ever heard Neil listen to, but it makes a bunch of people cry. I think he'd have liked something from Rush or Bob Dylan better. After that, the minister lets us know that the service will continue at the burial site and that we should follow the winding path behind the church up the hill. I cringe at the thought of Neil being lowered into the ground because it feels like burying my dad all over again. The choir starts singing a mournful hymn as people rise to their feet and begin filing out.

I see Neil's dad, his uncle, Vince and Marco, and some guy I don't know, along with Coach Turner, gather at the altar and I realize they're pallbearers. It's like a shot to the gut, not being asked to help carry his casket — his best friend. They didn't know him at all. It's like they're burying more than just Neil; they're burying a whole part of his life, the race life, with him.

Dean sees what I see and shakes his head. "That's not right," he says, his voice sounds rough, like bark. "You should be up there too."

"Thanks, man," I mumble.

We turn and file outside, the heavy music pulling our

heads down. On the lawn people are wiping tears or giving one another long embraces, while others get into their cars and drive away.

We start heading up the hill to the burial site, each step slow and deliberate. It feels like I'm dragging weights around my ankles.

"I don't think I can do this," Dean says.

Mags links her arm with his.

I stop halfway up the hill and tell them that I'll catch up with them in a minute, that there's something I need to do first. They nod and carry on. I draw my jacket tight against the cool wind and head toward my dad's grave.

When I reach his headstone next to the oak tree, I brush some small twigs and leaves off the top of it and read the plaque:

John Saunders
Loving dad
Played with bikes
Lived life to the fullest

I squeeze my temples before dragging my hand down along my face to dry the tears. I take a deep breath. I can't go through this again, but I don't have a choice. What's that John Lennon saying? *Life is what happens when you're busy making other plans.* I look at the plaque again. "I miss you, Dad." I clench my fist and place it on my chest, over my heart where I keep my thoughts for him.

I'm about to turn and leave when I see a miniature bottle of Canadian Club rye and a shot glass by the side of his headstone. There's a film of dirt on the glass, so I know it's been here for a while. My throat tightens. There's only one person who would have left that. Terry.

Friggin' hell, Terry, I think. You're killin' me.

I hear footsteps behind me, so I turn around. Wouldn't you know it, it's Terry. He sticks his hands into his pockets and looks at my dad's gravestone. "I'm sorry for what happened to Neil," he says. "He was another one of the good ones."

I look at my dad's plaque again. "Yeah, I'm sorry too," I say.

We stand there awhile, neither of us saying another word. There's so much history between him, my dad, me, and now Neil, and it's so god-damn awkward and complicated, and I don't have a clue why. A burning sensation hits my gut, filling me with this ache for things to be like they used to be. I fight spilling tears again.

"How come you don't come around anymore?" I say.

He bows his head apologetically. Says nothing.

I'd like it if he and I could just go for a beer or

something. But, I dunno, staring at the guy who won't even make eye contact with me makes me think too much time's passed or something. Maybe like Mags and me, some things are just too friggin' late.

"I thought we were like family," I mumble, then turn my back on him and start walking away. He calls my name, but I continue up the hill to where Mags and Dean stand huddled together. The minister positions himself at the head of Neil's casket and it's hard to hear what he's saying because we're pretty far back. The minister spreads his arms out with the palms facing up and everyone lowers their heads in prayer.

When I pull into the driveway, Dean's out of the truck before it can roll to a stop. He heads into the house and instead of slamming the garage door as usual, he lets it drift closed behind him.

Mags goes inside too. I walk around to the backyard, where I remove my jacket and tie, then lay them carefully across the back of a lawn chair. I roll up my sleeves and in the setting sun, I start chopping what's left of the woodpile. With every swing of the axe, every log that splits in two, I try not to think, but it's hard. I wish this heavy feeling in my gut would go away. Hell, I wish a lot of things, but I'm not going to get sucked into that pit again, not like when my dad died, when I just lay around the house all day not doing anything and being a bum. Of course, Neil helped me through it …

When the last of winter's cord is split and the sun's disappeared, I whack the blade into the chopping block and gather an armload of logs to take over to the firepit. The backyard light comes on, and Mags and Dean come out to join me. Without speaking, we get a fire going and sit around it and stare into the flames.

"All this doesn't seem real," Mags says, drawing the blanket she brought with her across her shoulders. "I keep thinking that I'm going to look up and see him come out that door." All of us glance up at the house, because she's right; we all want to see the impossible.

Dean sighs heavily like an old man ground down by too many years at the cannery. He pulls out a cigarette and pats his breast pocket for a lighter. When his smoke is lit, he draws long and hard on it like it's giving him some strength. "You know how Neil was kicked out of his house?" he says. "It was all 'cause of me." He exhales, and when he coughs, it sounds like an ice scraper scoring his throat. "He used his own money to bail me out of jail."

This news stuns me. I thought Neil moved out

because his folks wanted him to retire from racing and he needed his own space. No wonder he kept going on to me about letting Dean move in too. Neil was trying to save us all. Guess I was too far gone in my own misery to take two seconds to see what my best friend was going through.

"No one's ever helped me like that," Dean continues. "Not even my own family gave a shit." His eyes grow shiny in the fire's light. "He was my best friend." Dean half chokes, half sobs, then laughs like he's embarrassed and quickly wipes away a tear with the back of his hand. I stare at him. I had no idea just how much of an impact Neil had on his life.

I head into the kitchen for a second and return with a forty-ouncer of Crown Royal and three glasses. I crack the seal and pour us each a shot of rye.

"To Neil," I say, holding my drink out in front of me.

Dean and Mags stand too. "To Neil," they echo.

We sit back down and for a while we watch the logs burn, turning slowly into hot coals.

"I'll have to contact the TT organizers and cancel everything. Plane tickets, registration, homestay …" I say.

Dean coughs and spits a gob of phlegm onto the ground. "That sucks."

I nod, agreeing.

Mag sympathizes. "I'm sorry."

"Yeah, well. Sometimes life sucker-punches you."

Dean flicks his cigarette butt into the fire. "I think you should still go."

I look at him, startled, not sure if I heard him right.

"Why not?" he adds.

I shake my head. "I dunno. It doesn't seem right."

He reaches for another smoke. "I would. It's all he talked about. I'd go. I'd do it just for him."

I glance over at the tractor tires lying on the ground. New spurts of grass are doing a lousy job of camouflaging them. I think back to what he said about not having a chance at qualifying and how pissed off that made me feel.

"Yeah?" I say. "What if we all went?"

Mags turns from the fire and gives me a surprised look.

Dean's knee starts hammering up and down like a piston. "I don't have the funds, but you two should go, seriously."

I think of him getting turned down for that extra shift and how it was freely offered to me.

"Look, if you both want to go, I'll cover you. But you have to work the pits and, Mags, there's no chance in hell Vince and Marco are going now, which means you'll have to take lead. Think you can handle that?"

She nods, "Yeah, 'course I can."

I start nodding slowly. Dean just gives me this look, like a guy who, well, like a guy who's just been offered a chance to do something for his best friend and he can't believe it's happening.

He shakes his head. "Frig, you're yankin' my chain, man."

I get up out of my chair and hold my hand out for him to shake, letting him know I'm serious. He stands up and we shake.

I hold up the bottle of rye to the star-filled sky.

"To my dad and Neil, and to riding the TT," I say and let a stream of it pour onto the ground, sealing our pledge.

Dean and Mags drink to that.

I toss another log onto the fire, sit back down, and listen to the wood snap and pop. I draw in a deep breath and exhale. I feel like we've all just breathed for the first time in four days. Deciding to do this somehow makes the pain a little more bearable.

Not long after our pledge, some of our racing friends start dropping by. Mutton Chops, the owner of Goodman's, even a couple of old friends we'd hung out with in high school. I bring out more chairs and blankets, Mags puts more wood on the fire, and Dean heads inside to grab his guitar. We spend the evening half staring at the fire and half swapping stories about the guy we're all gonna miss like crazy. I get the chance to tell everyone what Neil had said about riding being nirvana, and we raise our glasses to that. When it grows quiet Dean lightly strums his guitar and starts playing "Dust in the Wind" by Kansas, something Neil would have liked.

chapter 7

That Monday, Dean and I hit the cannery floor ten minutes early so we can talk to Russ before our shift, but he isn't in his office yet. We kill time by doing pull-ups on the low-hanging pipe. Of course, Dean's got to try to do them faster than me and it becomes a competition. But it's hardly a contest when your opponent's face looks like a sweaty tomato after three pull-ups.

"Probably. Shouldn't. Smoke," he gasps.

I laugh and lose count.

"Hey," Russ shouts as he enters the cannery floor. "What did I say about doing that?"

We both let go of the bar and drop down.

"Just training Scott for the Isle of Man TT Races, Russ," Dean says.

Russ looks at me like I'm a lie-detector readout he

can get a bead on. "Well, do it on your own time, or the fish won't be the only thing getting canned around here."

"Hey, Russ," I say. "Can we talk to you for a minute?"

He gives a "come on, let's get this over with" hand gesture over his shoulder as he heads into his office. We follow and I shut the door. Same forgotten coffee cups, same plant on the ledge. He sits down and crosses his arms while Dean and I remain standing. My gut's screaming that our timing is all wrong and that we should just leave.

"So what do you boys want to talk about?"

Dean shifts his weight from one foot to the other. He's promised to keep his mouth shut and let me do the talking.

"Russ, we both have some vacation time," I say.

"Uh-huh." He opens the filing cabinet and pulls out my file, then he grabs Dean's, which is next to him. I wonder why it's so handy.

"Dean's got two weeks because he's been here longer, and I've got one week. But we'd like three weeks off each. The extra days without pay, of course."

"Three weeks?" He runs his finger across each page to confirm our start dates. "And when were you thinking of taking this time off?"

"Last week of May."

He shakes his head. "It's peak season. I need every hand on deck."

"I knew it," Dean mutters.

Russ looks at me. "Besides, you should have made this request back in January."

"But you always use temps in June for the extra work," I argue.

He raises one eyebrow as a warning not to be a smartass. "We hire temps to help with the packing and shipping. I don't use 'em on the line. If I did they'd all go home with missing digits. You two are just too valuable here. I'm sorry, it's a no."

"Figures," Dean grumbles.

"You see, Russ," I say, remaining calm, "we're going to the Isle of Man because I'm racing in the TT." Russ gives me that lie-detector look again, trying to spot the bullshit. "I was supposed to go with my dad. He and I talked about racing in it for years." I pause giving the information time to sink in. "I want to do this — for him." And for Neil, but I keep things simple. I wait for Russ's eyes to glaze over just like all the other times when my dad's name has come up.

Instead he lays his hands palms down on the desk and sighs. "Look, I wish I could help, but I can't."

My gut squeezes in on itself like a fist and I feel like I just dragged my dad's name through the mud. I was so sure it was going to work. Russ worshipped my dad.

He's always bragging that they'd once worked on the line together. What bullshit.

"Look, guys. A week in June maybe, but not three, and certainly not both of you at the same time."

Having nothing left to lose, I ask, "Would you let one of us go then, for three weeks?"

"Fine. Yes," he says, still looking at me, "one of you can go."

I glance over at Dean, who looks deflated. The night before, after working out in the backyard, I came around the side of the house to the garage. The door was open and there he was, standing in front of my race bike, removing the gas cap and setting it down on the ground by his right foot, then reaching for the funnel and an empty fuel jug. After counting to himself how long it'd take to refill my gas tank, he set everything down and picked up the gas cap, replacing it. He was pretending to fill up the tank. He was practising his pit job — by himself.

"Good," I say to Russ. "Dean's taking three weeks and today's my last shift. That should give you enough time to hire my replacement, eh?"

Now that I've quit Ferber's, I've kicked my training into high gear and use the time to double-check the checklists. One night, after a ten-klick jog and a post-workout shower, I come downstairs to find a stockpot of spaghetti and meatballs.

"Help yourself," Mags says.

Mags cooked? I tell her thanks and take a heaping plateful and walk into the living room with it, where she and Dean sit watching some old TT DVDs.

"So tell us more about this fourth you got to help us in the pits," I ask Mags.

"Her name is Branna Quiggin and she's Alan and Gwen's daughter."

I nod. Alan and Gwen Quiggin are the homestay people we're renting rooms from over there. They emailed the other day to say that they'd be happy to pick up my bike at the sea terminal and store the crate in their garage. They said they'd done this sort of thing plenty of times before with other racers' bikes.

"Branna's been part of several pit crews, changing visors and cleaning the windshields," Mags said. "She said she'd be happy to help out. Now, milestone thirty, name it."

"Verandah," I say.

Dean stares at the TV as he washes his spaghetti down

with a glass of milk. "Man," he belches, "Ian Hutchinson's recorded five wins. Dude's my hero."

I stick my fork into the pasta mountain and start twisting it, "Yeah, but Joey Dunlop will always be the best."

"Of course," Mags adds. "Goes without saying. Greatest. Rider. Ever."

"Sarah's Cottage's coming up next," I say.

"Okay, so is it just me?" Dean asks, putting down his empty plate. "Or, when someone mentions Sarah's Cottage, you picture a hot chick living there."

"No, Dean," Mags says. "It's just you."

"Huh. You sure?"

She swats him with a pillow and we laugh. Then a sharp guilt feeling hits my gut because we're having fun and Neil's not here. I tell myself that he would've liked seeing us getting along and joking around.

Dean slouches back into the sofa with a sudden stunned look on his face. "This is gonna be my first time out of the country."

"Really?" I ask, genuinely surprised for some reason. I glance at Mags. "I'll make sure she goes easy on ya."

It's a good thing the DVD cuts to a helicopter shot of the course, because it's the only way we could have heard the light tapping at the front door. We look at one another. It's obvious by our expressions that none of us is expecting visitors. Plus, no one ever uses the front door.

I get up and go answer it. Standing on the steps without makeup, hair pulled back, and wearing jeans and an oversize sweater is Cathy. She's got her arms crossed, but not in an angry way, more like she's trying to keep herself together. I knew this day was coming; I guess I just blocked it out.

"Hey," I say and pull her in for a hug because she looks like she could use one. After a moment she steps back and stares at her shoes.

"I — I thought I'd come by and get Neil's things … is that okay? Is this a good time? I — I can come back."

I open the door wide, inviting her in. Someone must have muted the DVD because it's quiet now.

"Hey," Cathy says and offers everyone a pained smile.

Mags gets up and gives her a hug. Dean stares at the TV.

It grows kind of weird in the room, like she's a total stranger or something, so she motions to the stairs and I follow her up.

"Neil's folks were going to come by," she says. "But I told them that I wanted to do it, that I insisted. Neil told me how they felt about him racing. I figured if I could do this for them, it'd be one less painful thing they have to go through."

When Cathy approaches Neil's door, she stops and I think it's because she can't bring herself to twist the knob and go inside. I know how she feels because I couldn't go into my dad's room for months. Neil was the one who stood next to me, helped me pack up his stuff, and rent out the room, which Mags now occupies. Neil was also there to wade through the estate lawyers, the bankers, the press. This is the least I can do for his girl. I reach for the handle and switch on the light. In one corner is a heap of clothes ready to be washed, on his dresser sits a basketball, and next to that, some pocket change. His bed's been left unmade, like he's just gotten out of it.

Cathy covers her face with her hands and I pull her in for another hug. I hold her until her breathing grows steady again.

"Did you have any boxes?" I ask.

She groans as if to say she's the world's biggest idiot.

I kiss her on the top of her head. "It's okay. Wait here." I head for the garage to grab some, and when I return, I find her lying in Neil's bed with the covers wrapped around her and his pillow clutched close to her chest, sobbing.

I don't know how long we were packing, but by the

time we load everything into her car it's dark outside.

Cathy looks around the garage at all our bikes. "What about his motorcycles?"

I write down and give her Terry's number. "He's a good guy," I say. "He'll look after you."

She gives me a hug. "Thanks, Scott, for helping me with this." She shuts the car's trunk. "You know his folks really don't blame you, right?"

I nod. "Yeah, I know. They're just sad and motorcycle racing is their punching bag."

Cathy puts on a brave face and smiles. "If you come across any other bike gear, do you think you can maybe donate it to someone who would like it? I think Neil would like that. He was always helping other people ..."

Neither of us speak. I know we're both thinking back to the night he died doing just that.

"Yeah," I say.

Cathy carries Neil's riding jacket over one arm as she walks back into the house. The TV's off and Dean's sitting doing nothing and Mags is surfing the Internet.

"You want a drink or something?" I offer. "Water, tea, beer?"

"No, thanks," she says and stares at her shoes. "I should go." I open the garage door for her because that's how all my friends come and go.

"Well, I guess I'll see you guys around sometime, huh?" she says.

Mags gets up and hugs Cathy. "I'll call you," she says.

Cathy tears up a little and it's sort of contagious, because I do too. "Come by anytime," I add and give her another hug. "You're always welcome here."

"Thanks, Scott."

Cathy looks at Dean. His knee hammers up and down. He still hasn't acknowledged that she's in the room.

"I know we never got along, Dean," she says. "But Neil always said that deep down you're a good guy."

He doesn't blink.

Cathy holds out Neil's jacket. "Here. I know he would have wanted you to have it."

Dean slowly gets up off the couch and takes the jacket from her. He stares down at it, then back at her. He's so touched by the gesture that he can't even say thanks, just mouths it.

From the front window we watch as she backs the car out of the driveway and then heads down the road. I meant what I said about her coming by anytime, but somehow I can't help but think that I'll probably never see her again.

I squeeze my temples. "I'm going to bed. I'll see you guys in the morning."

"G'night, Scott."

On the way to my bedroom, I look into Neil's old room. The bed's been stripped and the closet and drawers are empty. On the dresser there's a small stack of photographs. I pick them up and start going through them — house-party pictures, us at various races, and one that forces me to sit because I want to laugh and cry at the same time. Neil and I are about ten years old and we're at Goodman's standing beside our 60cc bikes and grinning because of our big, ingenious plan. We'd watched an Olympic swimmer on TV a few days before say that he'd shaved his head because it made him swim faster. Aerodynamics, he'd said. I chuckle, staring at our crewcuts. We look like army brats. Ah hell, we *were* brats. Man, those were some of the best times of my life. I take the photos with me, shut off the light, and close the door. In my room, I slide the photo of the two of us between the mirror and its frame so that it stays on its own. Then I run my fingers through my hair. There's one last thing I have to do tonight.

chapter 8

After a four-hour, twenty-minute flight to Toronto, then another ten hours to Dublin, stopping in Amsterdam, then backtracking, plus an additional two hours and fifty-five minutes on a Seacat ferry called *Manannan,* we finally arrive in Douglas, Isle of Man. By the time we dock, walk down the plank, and head for the terminal, we're exhausted and soaked to the bone. It rained the entire ferry ride over, so we saw nothing but fog, and the rough water had us fighting to keep our lunches down. Dean might have upchucked, I'm not sure. He disappeared and I wasn't about to leave my seat to go find him.

Mags shivers. Dean shoulders his guitar case so he can clutch Neil's leather jacket closer to him, like a second skin. I run my hands through my buzzed hair and wish I wore a heavier sweater. And they say Canada's cold. This place is freezing. It feels more like Vancouver in January, not the end of May.

The cars in the passenger pick-up/drop-off area fire up their engines as passengers hop in and take off. Soon it's just us standing under the overhang.

"You sure Alan knows when we're coming in?" Dean asks. "He didn't, like, mix up the time and think it was 2:00 a.m. instead of 2:00 p.m.?"

"Don't worry. Alan'll be here," Mags replies.

Five more minutes go by. Dean lights up a smoke. "I think we've been hosed."

Mags sits on top of her luggage, her feet barely touching the ground. "Dean, I seriously doubt they'd do that. You have to register with the Isle of Man government if you're going to provide a homestay. And I'm pretty sure the Quiggins wouldn't go through all that trouble just to 'hose' us."

Five minutes later, a dark blue van appears out of the mist and pulls into the lot. The driver's side window slides down and a guy in his forties, wearing a brown tweed jacket with the collar up, looks us over and smiles.

"Alan?" I ask and he nods. Sitting in the passenger's seat we see a girl around our age with long, wavy, brown hair and pale skin. It's probably Branna, I think, the one Mags mentioned was going to join our team.

"You must be the Canadians," he says, getting out of the van. We make quick introductions. Alan slides open the side door and I can see that the back's been modified with a bolted-in paddock bike stand. Handy, I think. This must be the vehicle Mags said we'd be using to transport my bike and gear while we're here.

Branna slips from the passenger seat into the back cargo space. "Hey, ya," she says and starts taking the luggage from us. From the way she handles our bags she's obviously stronger than she looks. I get a good feeling about her working in the pits.

"Sorry for the wait," Alan says. "I'm a bit shorthanded at the farm and needed to make sure we had the sheep secured."

Mags takes a seat in front with Alan and me. Branna insists that Dean take the seat in the back while she sits on a toolbox next to him.

"So you're riding in the famous TT?" Alan says.

"That's right," I say and a big *Oh my God, this is actually happening* wave rushes over me and I have to remember to breathe.

"We've had a few Canadians in the TT before," Alan goes on. "Pat Barns, Mike Duff, and Kevin Wilson, to name a few. I have to confess, if I had the skill and the nerves of steel, I'd do it myself."

Branna laughs. "Yeah, right, Dad. You can't walk and chew gum."

"Exactly why I stay put. So, it's the first time you lot have been to the Isle of Man?"

"Yeah," I say.

"Pity about the fog and rain. The thing to know about this place is that if you don't like the weather, wait twenty minutes and it'll change." He chuckles.

When we come to a roundabout, he taps his knuckle against the window. "Over there is where your TT course is. That's Quarter Bridge."

Roughly two klicks from the start, I think, and strain my eyes to see better, but all I catch is a few bales of hay and a telephone pole wrapped in thick, red safety padding. I'm so close to the course I can taste it.

"All your cargo arrived. I got it stored in the garage. I've got some tools there you can use. Just help yourselves."

"Thanks," Mags says.

I look over my shoulder. Dean's staring out the window. I try to imagine what it must be like for him being outside of Canada for the first time. The tiny white cottages nestled right up to the edge of the road must look quaint. The first time I went to England with my dad when he raced at Donington, I thought we had landed in the middle of a period film set.

"Is the race big in Canada?" Branna wants to know. "Do you see the TT on the news?"

"On specialty channels you do. We only have short circuits. They tried to get a Tourist Trophy started in Nova Scotia, but it got canned like an Atlantic salmon."

"Of course, you guys are big into hockey," Alan adds.

"Land of ice and snow," I say, shivering, and wonder if I've packed enough warm gear.

We turn onto a small side road that looks big enough for one car. Up ahead in the fog, I can see headlights coming our way. Alan doesn't seem fazed by it, he simply hugs the shoulder and the other car does the same. We pass, neither vehicle slowing down, and I find myself tensing up like a backseat driver. My knee even shifts to the side a little as if I'm on the bike about to kiss the ground rounding a corner. I smile despite myself.

"So," I say to Branna, "Mags tells me you've worked in the pits before?"

"Yeah. I helped Larry Carine last year at the Manx Grand Prix when his wife got sick and couldn't do it. Larry did quite well, didn't he, Dad?"

"He placed twenty-seventh."

"Which is really good, considering he's only raced it twice."

"*And* he's fifty-six years old. *And* a privateer."

Impressive. Then I realize that we too are considered privateers — self-financed as opposed to being backed by a manufacturer. Huh, I think. I haven't raced without sponsorship since I was twelve.

We turn onto an even smaller road, this one unpaved. It's just two bare strips of ground with grass growing up through the middle. I'm beginning to wonder what kind of place Mags has booked for us. I hope wherever we're going, they have electricity and indoor plumbing.

Something darts across the road in front of us.

"Was that a rat?" Dean asks.

"Oh, no, no, no. That's a long tail," Branna says quickly. "Or we call them Joeys."

"Huh," he says. "I could have swore a ra —"

"Long tail," Alan repeats, cutting him off. "There's no such thing as that other thing-that-shall-not-be-named on this island."

I laugh.

Eventually he brings the van to a stop. "This is it. Home sweet home."

I look up to see a barn.

We get out of the van, grab our luggage, and follow him and Branna past the barn along a high stone wall to where I'm happy to see a two-storey farmhouse.

Branna opens the front door and a Jack Russell tears

down the steps to greet us. It's so excited to see people that it circles everyone, then parks itself in front of Dean. Its tail wags so hard that its butt does the cha-cha. Dean bends down to pat it on the head.

"Hiya, boy."

"That's Pickles," Branna says. "She's a girl."

"Hiya, girl."

"Prettier than your last girlfriend," I say, stepping by him to head indoors.

"Don't listen to the big meanie," Dean whispers to Pickles. "He doesn't have a girlfriend."

Ouch, nice one, I think.

We bring the rest of the luggage inside and pull off our wet jackets and shoes. From the other end of the kitchen — which looks like something from *The Hobbit,* all cozy-like — a woman appears in a floral dress, wearing an apron and carrying a bunch of baby carrots in from the backyard.

"Hey, Mom," Branna says. "The Canadians are here."

She sets the carrots down on the counter and wipes her hands on her apron. "Hello, hello. Come on in. Make yourselves at home. I'm Gwen. It's nice to finally meet you. You must be Scott," she says, surprising me with a hug, then she turns to Mags. "Hello, Maggie," she says and hugs her too. She faces Dean. Oh god, I think.

"This handsome fellow must be Dean." He stands there stiff as a two-by-four as Gwen throws her arms around him. I try not to chuckle.

"Everyone, meet my wife," Alan says with comedic timing. We all laugh. Wait, do I see Dean blushing?

"Let me put the kettle on while you settle in," she chirps. "You must be exhausted and hungry. We'll have lunch in about half an hour."

Alan points to the stairs leading up to the second floor. "Take your pick from the rooms. The toilet's at the end of the hall."

"Thank you, sir." I have no idea why I'm talking all polite and stuff. Maybe it's to reinforce the polite Canadian stereotype. Just wait until Dean opens his mouth.

"You can call me Alan. This isn't the Queen's palace."

Gwen tells us that tea will be ready in about twenty minutes. Alan and Branna disappear outside while we head up a creaky set of stairs. I let Mags pick her room first and I take the one opposite hers. Dean takes the third one.

Before I enter my room, I get hit with this sad feeling, this sense of who's missing, Dad, Neil, and Terry. They should be here, I think. I push past the feeling because I don't want to bring the others down. "Hey," I say before they shut their doors to unpack their bags. They pop their heads out into the hallway. "Can you believe we're actually here?" I grin and a wave rushes over me, giving me a jolt like I've just downed an extra-large double-double. Then we all stand there grinning.

Mags hops into the shower first, and after I unpack and hang up my leathers, I walk across the wooden floor and look out the window. The fog's still thick and I can't see much, but I can hear sheep baaing in the fields.

Ten minutes later I leave my room to take a shower just as Mags is coming out of the bathroom. She's wrapped in a towel and has her neatly folded clothes pressed to her chest. Her wet hair falls in waves across her shoulders, and her pale pink skin and freckles make me search for somewhere safe to look.

"Hi," she says.

"Hey," I say to the rug.

"Let me know when you're ready to go downstairs and I'll go with you."

"Sure."

After I shower and change, I knock on her door and, thank god, she's in jeans and a sweater.

I knock on Dean's door, but there's no answer, so I open it. The room's empty. His guitar is on the bed and his jacket hangs on the back of a chair.

"Must be downstairs," I say. We head down to the

kitchen and I overhear something that startles me. I swear I just heard Gwen say, "Oh, Dean. You're quite a gentleman."

We enter the room to see her laughing and touching Dean lightly on the arm before turning to open the back door and ring a very loud cow bell. In the distance, Pickles starts barking.

"That's our dinner bell," she explains to us. Gwen picks up a plate of food from the counter and hands it to Dean, her new helper, and he carries it to a big dinner table.

I stare at him. "Who are you and what have you done with Dean?" I whisper so Gwen doesn't hear. The guy shoots me a look like I just knifed him. Man, why's he so sensitive all of a sudden?

"Settle in okay?" Gwen asks, and Mags and I nod. "Good. Let me know if you need anything."

I watch Dean set a plate of sausages down next to some scrambled eggs, bacon, beans, fried tomatoes, and potatoes.

"You're going to want to tuck in," Gwen says. "It'll go cold if we wait for Alan and Branna."

We take our seats just as the back door opens. Pickles comes charging in and stops right next to Dean.

"Ha," Alan says. "She knows who her favourite is,

don't you girl." He removes his jacket and washes his hands at the kitchen sink. Branna washes up after him.

When they sit, we all dig in.

Alan uses the side of his fork as a knife to cut into his eggs. "Bet you're anxious to see your bike."

Mags and I nod.

"Mags is a mechanic, Mum," Branna says.

Gwen's face lights up. "Oh? Don't get too many women mechanics, do we?"

Branna shakes her head. "Well, there's Jenny Tinmouth. She's a mechanic and TT rider."

"Do you race, Mags?" Alan asks.

"Nooo," she says with a laugh as if it were crazy talk, but I dunno. I think that if she were to train and wanted it badly enough, she could.

Alan sips his tea and looks at me. "Did Mags mention that you can use my old bike to get around the course?"

"She did," I say. "Thanks a lot. I really appreciate it."

"No trouble at all really. I'm afraid it hasn't seen the light of day in nearly a year, though."

That can't be good, I think. The dreaded barn disease: dead battery, seized callipers, carbs full of varnish sludge.

"That's not true, Dad. You had it out last October."

Alan nods. "Not much time to ride. The farm has me going day and night."

"We're short a helper," Gwen says. "He moved to London."

Alan nods. "The best time to learn the TT course, Scott, is to go out first thing in the morning. The earlier the better, so you won't run into any traffic. All you have to do is head back the way we came, take a left, and then a right and you're on it."

An hour later the fog has lifted and the sun is shining. Mags, Dean, and I follow Alan and Branna outside where he slides open the garage doors. Light spills across a three-by-six-foot wooden crate like something from an Indiana Jones movie.

We use a crowbar to open the crate and carefully unload the bike onto a paddock stand. Mags skillfully runs a hand over a couple of areas and lets her eyes scrutinize the rest.

I bend down to pick up some of the spare parts, neatly wrapped and taped with padding.

"It's okay, Scott. I've got this," Mags says.

I recognize the mechanic code for "Don't touch" and I get it. She doesn't want anyone messing with her checks and balances. Terry was the same way with my dad and me. He insisted on packing and unpacking everything himself.

"I can take you around the course in the van if you want, Scott." Alan says.

"Dad," Branna interrupts. "He doesn't want to go out with you in a van, he wants to go out on a bike."

It's exactly what I was thinking. I like this girl.

Alan leads us to the corner of the garage where he pulls back a blue tarp that covers his machine. "Well, it's no speed rocket, but it should help you get to know the road better."

I stare at his "old bike" with my gob open, ready to catch flies. It's a Triumph Trident T160, aka the "Slippery Sam." This model won the TT five years in a row back in its day.

Everyone, kindly move. I must ride — now.

"Picked her up ten years ago at an auction," Alan says. "Paid an arm for it, but don't tell the missus. She thinks I got it at a rummage sale."

"What's the mileage?" I ask.

"Only done twenty thousand from new — she's barely run in."

Mags comes over to check out the bike. "Wow. Look at all that chrome."

I leave them to talk megaphone exhaust and how

much rejetting the bike requires as I all but run back to the house to change into my leathers and grab my helmet and gloves. When I return, Alan's already got the bike started and she's humming all throaty like Janice Joplin.

I'm about to ride a Triumph Trident. Cross that off the bucket list.

I ride along the gravel drive, back the way we came in, take a left and then a right, like Alan said. The Trident's engine hums, and feels strong and stable, like she's still got plenty of kick still left in 'er. The narrow, almost flat handlebars are comfortable under my grip. It's easy to see how, in its day, this machine gave genuine superbike performance.

I slow to a stop at the end of the road and touch my riding boot onto the asphalt. The next turn I make I'll be on the TT course. Chills run all over my body and I feel wide awake. The names of TT legends start running through my head: Stanley Woods, Geoff Duke, Mike Hailwood, Giacomo Agostini, Steve Hislop, David Jefferies, Bob McIntyre, John McGuinness, Joey Dunlop, and more.

I lift my foot and slowly open the throttle.

chapter 9

My alarm goes off at 4:00 a.m. island time. The jet lag is nasty and for a second I'm not sure where I am. I haul my butt out of bed before I nod off again. I want to get in four laps before traffic clogs up the roads. Four laps a day over the next six days gives me twenty-four times around the course before practice week starts.

I grab a quick bite, then head out. Being on the TT course for the first time yesterday was like déjà vu — all the TT video games and onboard DVDs I'd watched — but then again, it wasn't. I had no idea how massive one lap is. Sure, I know it's sixty kilometres (or thirty-seven and three-quarter miles in imperial measure), but every ten minutes that pass and I see all those villages, hills, bends, and turns, all I can think is *Damn, I'm still on lap one!* I can't easily mind-map this course like I can the smaller race tracks. Top riders say it takes three years to learn your way around here before you can even *think* of placing anywhere near the top ten, let alone the winner's podium. Three years, man. I'm awestruck and suddenly jacked that I get to hit the course at racing speeds next week.

I'm not timing my laps when I'm on the Triumph because I'm not on my race bike and the course is still a regular island road. Sure there are sections without speed limits like around the Cronk-y-Voddy and on the mountain stretch, but I just want to get the lay of the land, take in all that street furniture, and get used to driving on the opposite side of the road. They have signs all over the place for the German tourists who come here during the TT that say *links fahren* — drive on the left — because Germans drive on the same side of the road as we do in North America.

On my third lap I take a mental snapshot of the four checkpoints on the course and brand them into my brain. The first is at Glen Helen, the one-quarter-way mark. The halfway point is the Quarry Bends. The Creg marks three-quarters, and the fourth's at the grandstand.

The section I seem to be gravitating toward and learning the fastest is the stretch between Brandywell and just past Creg-ny-Baa in the third quarter.

On my last lap, just past the Highlander Pub, a guy on a touring bike with UK plates catches up to me. When we reach the top of Creg Willey's Hill and see that it's traffic-free for a good stretch, we kick it up a notch. He blows past me, taking the turns with confidence, and I get the feeling that I'm not the only racer out for an early morning spin. I take it up to 90 and watch as he leans to the far right before taking the next series of downward bends with ease — car-free from the other direction, of course. He rides like he knows his way around. In the slower section, near Kirk Michael, he points his finger before taking the corner and that's when I realize he's showing me the apex on the bend.

We ride like this for the rest of the lap and when we come up to the grandstand on Glencrutchery Road, he stands up on his pegs and pumps his fist high into the air like he's just won the Senior TT. I laugh and get up onto my pegs too. I feel the wind pressing hard against my body as I imagine the roar of the crowd. What a rush.

The morning island traffic slows us down and we both pull into the gas station at the top of Bray Hill to fill up. I pull my bike in behind his.

He lifts his visor and a patch of silver bangs frames his forehead. "Nice morning for a ride," he says in a thick English accent. He opens his gas cap and fills up the tank.

I totally recognize his icy-blue eyes. He's Paul Parker, six-time TT champ, winner of multiple Junior and Senior races, and hails from a racing family dynasty. He's placed on the podium eighteen times. Dude's a legend.

"Sure is," I say and reach over to fill up my tank while I try not to look starstruck. "Just getting to know the course," I add.

"You a TT rider, then?"

I nod and offer my hand. "Scott Saunders."

"American?"

I shake my head. "Canadian."

He raises his eyebrows in surprise and returns the gas nozzle to its holster so he can shake my hand. "Well, I knew you must be a rider. Your leathers don't match the bike."

I look at the classic T160, then chuckle at my red-and-black outfit.

"I was just out myself," he says, "reliving a bit of the glory days and saying hello to some old friends. Don't get too many Canadians in the TT. How are you getting on?"

My cheeks puff out as I exhale a big breath slowly.

"Ah, don't worry. Take your time. Took me years to know it. Want my advice?"

I'd be stupid to say no.

"Pick a section, a couple of miles stretch, and know

it like the back of your hand, then add more to it each time you're out."

Makes sense.

"Got a familiar spot yet?" he asks.

"Sulby Straight," I say, half joking and half not.

He chuckles. "It's nice through there. When the wind's at your back, you can get up to one-ninety. Has anyone shown you the course yet?"

I shake my head. "Newcomers' briefing isn't until Saturday."

Five days and twenty more times around.

"Well, I'm only in town until tonight. I have to head back to London for my daughter's wedding next week, but I'd be happy to give the course another couple of goes after something to eat, if you'd like."

A rush spreads through my body faster than a smile can appear on my face. A retired champ showing me the course. How awesome is that? "That'd be sweet," I say and add that I'm paying for breakfast.

We go for a bite at a pub in Union Mills. He recommends this dish called queenies, so I order it. Turns out to be scallops freshly caught this morning and sautéed in garlic with little strips of ham, chock full of protein. I'm instantly addicted.

Paul wipes his mouth and pushes his empty plate

aside. "You know, people say the bottom of Bray Hill is the ultimate challenge for bravery. But it's not; it's the top. The crossroads at St. Ninian's is the point of no return and at 160 mph it's like going off the edge of the world. There's no feeling quite like it. We call it 'The gates of Armageddon. The road to hell.'"

A free-falling sensation hits my gut like I'm already there. I exhale and relax my shoulders.

"The main thing is to set up your bike for stability," he says. "Otherwise, your brain won't let yourself go fast over the bumps and jumps."

"Stability," I say, nodding.

"Now, the top and bottom of Bray Hill are easy compared to the top and bottom of Barregarrow. Don't drift too wide there."

"Right, Barregarrow. Don't drift wide."

"Take the slow corners slow. There're only a handful of first- and second-gear bends. Make up the time on the fast sections."

"Fast on the fast. Slow on the slow."

"Just ride as if you're late for work."

"Late for —" I look up at him and see that he's pulling my leg.

"Just relax, Scott. Remember, this should be fun."

Huh, I think. Easy for him to say.

I get on the back of Paul's badass-but-comfortable touring bike so that each time we come to a roundabout or a restricted zone, we can flip up our visors and he can talk me through the course.

"Make sure whenever you're travelling around the island that you only go one way if you're on this road. Don't drive the opposite direction. It'll mess you up. Also, try to follow someone in practice who's a little faster than you for a few corners, then let them go. Don't ride anywhere near the limit."

We head through Quarter Bridge and out of Douglas. Paul points to an empty field. "Next week it'll be full of campers barbecuing, so you'll smell sausages and hamburgers. Try not to let it distract you." Further on, he points to a parking lot up ahead. "Use this lay-by as a marker. Get over to the right and it'll help set you up for the right following this left corner. Come into it late, keep to the left, and drive out of the right-hander hard.

"Get the bends at Union Mills right and you'll carry your speed all the way to Greeba Castle. That's about three kilometres flat out with just Ballagarey, a very fast right-hander, to master. It's a 150 mph in fifth gear. It takes a bit of nerve, it's faster than you think, but you have to build up to it. We don't call the corner Ballascary for nothing."

Ballascary?

On the faster sections where we can't talk, Paul points his finger to the apex in the turn or holds his hand out parallel to the ground and either raises or lowers it in a quick dipping motion to indicate when a jump's coming up and if the bike's front or back end will land first. The Cronk-y-Voddy straight is one of those sections with a large series of undulations, which, at 160 mph, means I'd be grabbing more air time than asphalt.

We ride on, but get stuck behind a double-decker bus until it's safe to pass. Paul points to a parking lot up ahead. "Now keep on it past the Highway Board yard. Watch the front wheel, as it'll go airborne just before dropping into fifth gear for the right and down again for the following tight left, then come in late and accelerate hard for this next quick section."

I have no idea how I'm going to keep all this straight.

He slows the bike down to thirty as we approach the village of Kirk Michael, and we flip up our visors.

"In this corner, you're going to come in right by the curb early on, clip it. The bends up ahead are deceiving. Take the straight line through them. You've got to be right on point. Miss one corner around here and you'll get the next six wrong just sorting yourself out."

After ten minutes and getting stuck behind some more traffic, he shouts, "You smell that?"

I inhale a deep breath. The air smells earthy, pungent, and kind of sharp. "Is that garlic?"

"Wild garlic." He points along the side of the road where it grows.

"When you smell that, you know you're coming up to the town of Ramsey."

We do two more laps and each time small sections are becoming more familiar, but then he adds a hundred more things to remember. Over two hundred and something bends. It's like I'm drowning. One thought hits me, hard: I could die here.

He shows me the places where he's come off the course and been taken by helicopter to Noble's, the island's hospital. He also points out where he lost a lot of riders he knew, and I get chills. Now I understand what he meant when he said he'd been out this morning saying hello to old friends.

After our lap, Paul drops me off at the pub. My brain's mush. I want to thank him a million times, but he's already told me to stop doing that.

"I'll be gone practice week," he says, "but I'll be listening on the radio and I'll return on the weekend after that. Good luck, Scott." He shakes my hand.

"Thanks a lot, eh." I get on my bike and start it up.

"Oh, and one last thing," he says. "Keep the sea to your left, keep the rubber side down, and if you see a cow, don't hit it."

I laugh and for a moment, it feels like the burning in my gut is out of the red line. Paul pulls out onto the road, gives me a wave, and drives out of sight. What a cool guy.

I return to the Quiggins' farm at around one-thirty. No one's in the house and I'm too bagged to check on Mags and see how she's doing with the bike, so I park myself in my room on my bed. My ears are ringing and I feel a headache coming on. It's like I got my ass handed to me today. There's so much I gotta learn.

I wake up three hours later to the sound of laughter outside. I climb out of bed and look out the window. Dean and Branna are strolling across the field as Pickles runs circles around them. Dean's chewing on a blade of grass and he's throwing his hands all over the place. I can't hear what he's saying, but she's laughing again. I wonder if something's wrong with her; she thinks the guy's hilarious.

I head out to the garage. I'm pumped about telling Mags that I met Paul. All of her tools and gear are laid out neatly and it looks like she's been working on the clutch. I see her leaning against the bench and staring at the ground.

"Hey," I say.

She looks up. "Hey, Scott."

"You okay?"

She half shrugs, but her eyes say no. "I just got an email from the bi-pedal carbon-based parental units. They were going to fly out and see me — probably wanted to drag me back to Toronto — so I had to tell them I was here. They took a colossal fit."

I wince as if I've been physically burned.

"'We didn't send you money to quit school and traipse halfway across the world,'" she says, imitating them. "They said that if I wasn't going to university, then they wanted their money back — with interest."

"Ouch. So what are you going to do?"

She folds her arms across her chest. "I dunno. I don't really want to talk about it."

But she goes on, "I'm already here. It's not like there's anything they *can* do about it." She picks up a wrench and points it at my bike. "You know, this is all I want to do. I don't want to be an economics major."

"So keep doing it." Why not? I think. It's not the easiest life and the average race mechanic isn't loaded — let's just say they do it for the love of it — but hell, if she plays her cards right, a big team will scoop her up, she can see the world, and eke out a decent living.

"You know what?" she asks.

"What?" I say.

She shakes her head and looks back at the bike. "Never mind. I don't want to talk about it."

Wow, she's not exactly an open book. "So how's the bike coming?" I ask, changing the subject.

"Good. I'll have it finished by Thursday. How's the course? You were gone a long time."

"Yeah," I say, and I want to tell her how massive it is, but change my mind. She's already bummed out about her own problems and I don't need to add mine to it.

"Hey, you'll never guess who I met," I say, letting a grin spread across my face.

Her face lights up and that gleam I like returns to her eye. "Who?"

chapter 10

"Dude, you look like shit."

I slap Dean on the shoulder as I climb the stairs to my room. "Thanks, man. Don't hold back, eh."

He chuckles, and I gather that none of the Quiggins are in earshot of Mr. Potty Mouth.

It's Thursday. Day four. Sixteen times around and eight more to go until the first official practice lap on Sunday. Tiny hairs on my forearms rise just thinking about it. Every day it's up at four to put in four laps and then head back to the farm. Then it's sleep, eat, study the course, go for a five-klick jog, check on how the bike's doing, eat, make small talk, review notes, run the course through my head, go to bed, and repeat. As the week goes on, it takes me longer to get in my morning runs because the road is growing clogged with bike fans on pilgrimages from all over the world. I've spotted plates from Germany, Italy, France, Ireland, Scotland, England and Wales, even Australia, and South Africa. Can't say I blame them for getting up early too and wanting to get a taste of the most famous mountain circuit in the world.

I shut my bedroom door, peel off my leathers, and fall into bed. Since I got up this morning, I've been feeling a little off camber. I think what I need is a good nap.

I wake up a few hours later still feeling like crap, so I decide to skip my run. I take a shower and check in with Mags. I find her listening to Manx Radio TT 365 and safety-wiring the race bike to make sure nothing loosens and flies off.

"Hey," I say.

She looks up from her work.

"Hey. How's it going?"

"Okay."

She tilts her head to one side. "You sure? You don't look so hot."

"Thanks," I say. I guess I'm not well because I get sarcastic when I'm sick.

She puts down the safety-wire pliers and gets in close to me like I'm a patient and she's a doctor, or better yet, a nurse.

"I can see why Dean thinks you've been working too

hard. You look pale. Your eyes are bloodshot."

"Huh." I'm surprised I'm even on the guy's radar. "Where *is* the Deaner?"

"Hanging with Branna."

I raise my eyebrows.

"I know, I know," Mags says and turns back to the safety-wiring. "Right now he's helping her with some sheep-herding stuff."

We both must be picturing the same thing — Dean all awkward around farm animals — because we start laughing at the same time.

"Must be love if he's working without pay," I joke. "I don't know whether to be happy for the guy or wonder what's wrong with her."

Mags swats me lightly on the shoulder. It shouldn't hurt, but it does; it stings.

"The bike is pretty much set for Sunday's first practice. You excited?"

My stomach does a flip and I smile. *The gates of Armageddon. The road to hell.* I crouch down and check the tension on the bike's chain. "Can't be too tight or too loose," I say, remembering what Paul said about stability.

She takes a swig from her water bottle. "What time do you want to head over to the paddock on Saturday to set up?"

"Seven or eight sounds good. There's a newcomers' briefing at noon and I want all of us there." I can't tell if the chain's right because I just realized that you need to sit on the bike to check the tension. I must be sick. My body sways a little like I'm standing on a waterbed. "I think I'd better go back to bed. I'll probably skip dinner. Tell Gwen and Alan, will you?"

She nods. "I think that's a good idea."

I mull over a self-diagnosis as I stand there. I think I've overdone it by getting up at 4:00 a.m., sleeping during the day, then training hard. "I should take tomorrow off." It just about kills me to say that because my mind is willing, but my body is not.

"You know what you need?" she says.

You rubbing my back until I fall asleep, I think. "What's that?"

"Get your mind off all this for a day. Let's do something, go somewhere. The only place I've been to is this house, the garage, and a ferry ride in the fog."

I nod. "Okay. Tomorrow we'll do the tourist thing."

Sometime in the night I wake up in a sweat, like I've just broken a fever or something. I take it as a good sign.

Maybe I caught a twenty-four-hour bug or maybe I've been overtraining.

We end up getting a late start on our tour day. A ram and a bunch of ewes escaped before Alan discovered a gate was unlocked, and he needed Branna's help rounding them up again. The local radio plays public service announcements nonstop for the tourists telling them that if they explore the countryside, make sure all gates are closed. The last thing a TT rider needs is to be flying down the road, doing 190 mph and have a herd of sheep wander on the course.

We finally assemble and pile into the van. "You ready for the TT?" Branna asks. I volunteer to sit in the back as Dean and Mags get into the front with Branna.

The mere mention of the race makes me want to bail on our little excursion, and I have to remind myself that today's a recovery day. Besides, Dean and Mags are all smiles and joking around.

"Can never be too ready," I answer.

"Well, the first thing we have to do is say hello to the fairies."

I wait for Dean to make a crack, but he doesn't.

"Oh sure," Branna says, "there's the fairy bridge on your way to the airport, but there's another one, a secret one."

I raise one eyebrow at Dean, but he's looking all doe-eyed at our tour guide.

"You can't come to the Isle of Man and not say hello to the little people," she explains. "It's considered bad luck to pass over the bridge without saying, 'Good morning, fairies,' or 'Good afternoon, fairies,' or 'Good evening, fairies.' People even leave messages on little pieces of paper with wishes on them."

I chuckle, shaking my head. A fairy-loving girl is going to be a part of my pit crew. This should be good. As long as she travels clockwise whenever we're on the course today, I don't care what we do. I am a tourist monkey.

As they chat in the front, I check out the scenery. Endless patchwork of rolling fields, all bordered in a mustard-coloured prickly bush called gorse. We pass the occasional *tholtan* — one of the original stone farm-houses or cottages, deserted now, that dot the country-side. Dean taught me that word. He must have learned it from Branna, because the Quiggins have a tholtan on their property. The Isle of Man is like going back in time, except for all the motorcycles on the road, which are making me twitch a little. I tell myself to settle down. Remember, tourist monkey.

We head for old Castletown Road towards a place called Quine's Hill. After a few minutes Branna slows down to tap on the window just like her dad did the night we arrived. "Here we are," she says and pulls off to the side of the road. We pile out and follow her, crossing the road and past someone's barn toward the woods. After twenty minutes of walking a narrow dirt road better suited to rubber boots and a walking stick than sneakers, we eventually come to a stream and a tiny wooden bridge. Branna takes us to the right of the bridge and as we continue along the bank, I spot tealight candles and sun-faded plastic flowers. Then I see an old stone bridge overgrown with ivy and it's like something out of a children's picture book. Hundreds of little coloured envelopes sealed in plastic baggies either rest under small stones or are tucked into the joints of the stonework. It's well-known that a certain TT rider always visits the fairy bridge before each race. Hey, everyone's got their superstitions. Even Valentino Rossi. He has to put one boot on before the other, put one glove on before the other, and sit on his bike the same way every time. Heck, I'm no one to talk — I've got my own race thing.

"Moghrey mie Mooninjer Veggey," Branna says, then translates it for us. "Good morning Little People." She looks at us. "Come on, everyone, you've got to say it."

We try our best but make a garbled disastrous mess of it.

Branna smiles and pulls a pen and four pieces of paper from her pocket for us to write down our wishes. I feel kinda dumb at first, but like they say, when in Rome, do what the Romans do.

We write down our wishes and tuck them between the stones that make up the bridge.

I guess Dean must have told Branna about us working at Ferber's, because our next stop on the tour is the kipper factory in Peel. You'd think Dean and I would be sick of the fish scene, but we don't mind watching the smoking process, and the smell of smoked fish gets our mouths watering. We eat some kipper on fresh bread they call *baps* for lunch, and when Dean lights up a post-meal cigarette, Branna pulls it from his lips and grinds it into the gravel with the heel of her boot. They mock-argue for a bit and I guess she wins the argument because he doesn't reach for another smoke.

"Did you tell Scott and Mags that you're doing the Ramsey Sprint next week?" Branna asks Dean.

Mags and I look at him.

"Yeah, I'm doing the Ramsey Sprint," he says.

"What's that?" Mags asks.

"It's a drag strip," he says. "One-eighth of a mile, fast as you can."

I guess it's for the tourists, I think. So they too can

feel the experience of going flat out. "You riding Alan's bike?" I ask.

"Yup."

Poor guy won't have much of a machine left by the time we're done with it.

On the way back to the van, Mags stops to pet a brown cat that runs up to her. We all notice that it's missing a tail.

"That's one of the famous Manx cats," Branna says. "They have no tails. This one's a Rumpy," she adds. "Different from a Stumpy, Riser, or a Longy."

I have no idea what she's talking about. I just hope she knows what she's doing in the pits.

"Do you know the story behind their tails?" Branna asks. Dean shakes his head like a preschooler at storytime. "Well, when Noah was calling all the animals to board the Ark, the cats were nowhere to be seen and just as he was about to close the hatch, in they jumped, but the doors cut off their tails."

Dean and Mags laugh, but I don't. I'm feeling jumpy now, and like I want to head back to the farm to study my notes.

We pile into the van and end up on the TT course again, which calms me down because I can look out the window and identify some course markers. When we reach the Bungalow, Branna pulls off at a rest stop so we can visit Joey Dunlop's memorial. We get out and zip up our coats against the strong winds. The life-size statue of Joey smiles at us as he sits on his bike overlooking the Bungalow Bend at Snaefell. It gets me thinking about my dad and Neil. I wish they were here to see this too. I look at my pit crew as they joke around and my gut gets all knotted up. Mags has travelled halfway across the world and spent money that she doesn't have to prove to herself and her folks that she can do this for a living. And Dean? I'm betting he won't have a job when he gets back because there won't be any more thefts at the cannery while he's away, which'll mean that all fingers will point to him. He'll get served a pink slip. I can just see it. I shove my hands in my pockets and walk away from Joey's smiling face. If I don't qualify for this race, I'll have let a lot of people down.

"Right where we're standing on Snaefell Mountain," Branna says, "is the island's highest point."

Two thousand, thirty-six feet, I think.

"Snaefell is Old Norse for 'snow mountain' and from here you can see the seven kingdoms of heaven." She raises her hand and points them out. "Scotland, England, Wales, Ireland, Mann, the Kingdom of Heaven, and the Kingdom of the Sea."

I take a good long look. It's the first time I've drunk in the scenery even though I've been driving by here all week.

"Sure is beautiful," Mags says. I see over my shoulder that Dean and Branna are kissing. It makes me uncomfortable because I don't have the guts to find out if Mags still likes me and now's not a good time because I don't want rejection on my plate either.

"Aww, puppies and kittens," I say loud enough to make everyone laugh.

We pile back into the van. "What do you guys want for dinner?" Branna asks.

I'm hoping we head back to the farm.

"I want to try some of the more exotic cuisine on the Isle," Mags says.

"I can see seven places from here," I mumble from the back seat. "The pub, the pub, the pub, the chip shop, the pub, the pub, and the pub."

We head for the Douglas Promenade. It's getting harder to play tourist monkey and I have to remind myself that soon there won't be any time off, so I should just suck it up and enjoy myself. We find a parking spot on a side street and stroll along the sidewalk. There must be more than a thousand bikes cruising or parked along the prom.

"The way men stop midstep to ogle the bikes, you'd think they were naked women," Branna comments.

"Yeah, total bike porn," I add, smirking, then stop to check out all kinds of European bikes I don't get to see in North America, bikes like the Velocette Venom, a single-cylinder four-stroke British bike.

We find a place to eat and I introduce Dean and Mags to queenies, which we all agree are awesome. After that we walk along the promenade and check out the fun fair, watching the kids try not to puke on a ride we've nicknamed The Vomitnator. We eventually end up at Bushy's Ale of Man, an outdoor tent. Everyone grabs drinks. I sit back in my white plastic chair next to Mags, sipping my ginger ale and watching Dean as he makes friends with strangers, which is an unusual sight to see. More than once he points me out in the crowd and I think he's telling everyone he's in the TT and that I'm the rider.

"I feel like Dean thinks all this is one big laugh," I say to Mags.

We watch as Branna interlaces her fingers with Dean's.

"I don't think he finds it funny," Mags says.

"Okay, maybe not funny ha-ha, but I don't think he's taking this seriously. Does he know what he's doing in the pits?"

"Yeah. I trained him."

I down the rest of my drink. "Well, it's one thing to practice in the garage, and it's another to be able to do it on race day with riders flying by at 180 klicks, thousands of people watching, technical inspectors on your case, and press with lenses strong enough to see into your skull."

She all but waves me off. "Don't worry about it. He's ready."

"I hope so."

"Back off, sergeant. He'll be fine. Relax, will you? You're too tense."

I pull a "Mags move" and bluntly stop talking about it.

We finally get back to the farm where I fall into bed. When I shut my eyes, I can still see the neon fun-fair lights swirling in my head and the sound of kids shrieking. I try to switch it over to the TT course, but it's not happening.

chapter 11

I wake up feeling physically better, but now the only headache I've got is my crew. I turn the van down the last lane of the paddock. "Man, we should have got here earlier," I say. We agreed to head out at 7:00 a.m., but it's 7:45 before I get Mags's and Dean's hungover butts out of bed. Then we have to wait for Branna, because she's helping Alan out with some kind of sheep thing. *Then* she tells us she'll meet up with us later because she has to make up for the chores she skipped out on yesterday. If I'd known that would happen I'd have skipped the island tour and helped Alan myself.

We're assigned to Paddock C, which is basically a gravel parking lot. The grassy Paddocks A and B are closer to the grandstand, the warm-up area, and the technical-inspection station — basically everywhere you want to be within close reach. Only guys with big sponsorship backing get these prime spots for maximum exposure, and we privateers get to tough it out in the trenches. Personally I think it's the privateers who are the real heart of every race. Anyone who has to work twice as hard, scrimping and saving for their passion, gets my full respect. Of course, I wouldn't turn down a chance to race a custom-built state-of-the-art machine that came with a crew of ten, a massage therapist, and a chef either.

"Well, it's official," Mags says. "We're the last spot in the last row. "Hurray," she adds, trying to make light of it.

To add insult to injury, a car drives by and kicks up a dust cloud, causing a few stones to bounce our way. No one says it, but I think we can all agree that it's major suckage.

We get out of the van and are greeted by blasting opera music, courtesy of our new neighbour. We don't know what to say or think, so we focus on getting our paddock set up.

I pop open the van's back doors. "How do you want this set up, Mags?"

"Well, first pull out the gearboxes," she says. "Set that one here, that one there." She points and Dean and I snap to it like a couple of delivery guys. We assemble the easy-up shelter, lay down an old piece of carpet Gwen gave us, and when Mags arranges our personal pit space to her specifications, I go and introduce myself to our neighbours. The opera guy is Karl Schmidt from somewhere in Germany. That's about all I could understand from his thickly accented English. What I do know is that Karl's got this huge honking leg of smoked lamb — or pig or goat, I dunno — that's been jerry-built to something resembling a lathe I once used in high school shop class. Every now and then he stops working on his bike, pulls out a knife, lifts up the cheesecloth covering, and slices off a hunk of meat. When he sees us watching him — okay, staring — he takes a bite and smiles big, showing us his toothy grin, then offers his knife to us. I tell Dean to go for it, but amazingly, even he's not that stupid. Our neighbour on the other side, also next to the exit road, is Garth Myers from Spratton, England. While he works away to the operatic sounds, his wife, Jean, balances a bawling baby on one hip while stirring a pot of beans and sausages over a hot plate. It makes me look pretty pampered in comparison.

We kill time before the newcomers' meeting by taking a tour of the other paddocks. The set-ups around us are pretty basic, like ours, but the closer we get to the grandstand the bigger and flashier things get. Huge tour buses serve as backdrops for the equally large work tents, some of which house up to five race bikes and a crew of four to ten mechanics. We stand behind a purple velvet rope in front of one tent watching a half-dozen mechanics in new, custom-fit team clothing work for a bit. Everything is pristine and tidy. They don't even have to kneel on the grass — they've got thick interlocking carpet under their feet. No dust clouds here.

Dean whistles. "Dudes are armed to the tits."

"Yeah," I say. "Blow a $36,000 superbike engine and no problem, just throw in your spare or, hell, grab your backup bike. A privateer blows an engine and it's game over."

"That's gotta suck," he comments. "What are the chances of blowing an engine?"

Mags tears her eyes away from the superbike for a second. "Anything can happen." She refocuses on a mechanic who's working on the mega-dollar factory machine tricked out with unobtainium parts. A short, stocky older guy with a bulbous nose and the name Arnie written on his overalls sees her. He nods a friendly hello and she returns the gesture, her eyes still on the machine. "Even these bikes can break down, throw a rod, blow a chain," she says. "Plus, they break down more often because they're highly stressed."

"What happens if something goes wrong with your bike?" Dean asks me.

"It won't," Mags answers.

"All this way for nothing," I say to him.

Dean whistles. "Knock wood."

I rap on his head twice and he laughs a second later when he gets the joke.

I pass out our official laminated TT badges with lanyards, which grant us access to all the restricted areas, including the Race Office and Meeting Room, the next place we need to go for the newcomers' meeting. On our way there, we pass the famous Shuttleworth Snap — a replica of the motorcycle the character George Shuttleworth rode in the 1935 TT movie *No Limit*.

The Meeting Room buzzes with this electrical charge and tiny hairs on my arm stand up. There's a lot of talk and the occasional fake peal of loud laughter. I take a rough count of twenty-five people, even though there are only twelve newcomers this year. I guess I'm not the only new rider who's brought along crew. The three of us take a seat in the back row and pick up a set of handouts that lie on each chair. In the row ahead of me is a guy I'd swear looks fifteen, but you have to be eighteen by the end of May to qualify. I also see a Japanese guy talking to one of the officials through a female interpreter. Man, here I am, someone who speaks English, riding the toughest road course in the world, one that takes three years to learn; I can't imagine doing it in a country where I can't speak the language and I have to rely on a translator.

Another organizer, a friendly blond guy with glasses, claps his hands in the international gesture of "Okay, it's time to shut up and listen up." He says, "Right. I'm Roger Morgan," and we all recognize who he is. He's been our contact all the way through the registration process, sending us emails and other important information. He's done a lot for us. He even sent his condolences when he heard about Neil.

"Welcome, everyone. It's good to see you. We're holding this briefing because we'd like to say hello to each of you and go over some important information. So let's get started, shall we?"

Roger signals to another guy, who cuts the lights and brings up a slideshow. He starts by going through a series of changes to the course that we wouldn't find on any video game, like the grippy road surface at the Bungalow and the natural spring that can cause wet patches even on dry days.

"We're on an island in the middle of the sea, so fog and mist can come up, low clouds can come down easy as ever. At the startline, we'll show you a matrix board with as much information on it as we can put about the road conditions around the course. It might say that there are wet roads in the Ramsey area or low cloud on the mountain or Cronk-y-Voddy."

He goes on to mention that our first speed-controlled lap will take place on Monday. This is a guided lap for newcomers only. They'll split us into four groups of three and we'll follow a travelling marshal — usually an ex-champ — for one lap. After we finish the lap, they'll remove our training wheels, so to speak, and we're on our own for three more laps as they let the other eighty or so other riders onto the course for their chance to practice.

"Do not pass the Travelling Marshal," Roger says, which makes everyone chuckle. Who would be stupid enough to do that? But I guess if he has to say it, it's probably happened.

Next he shows us a detailed slide of the pits. This is what I need Mags and especially Dean to see. I look over at Dean and find him slouching in his chair.

"Now, there are a hell of a lot of bodies in pit lane with two or three people in each stall jumping out to help you or your fellow competitors, so be careful. It's not like a Formula One race — it's very tight in there.

As you ride in, stay in the middle until you get to your pit number, and as you leave, accelerate and cross over to your left side and get out of the way of the people coming in. During practice week there is no refuelling from the tanks, but you can practice your pit stops, get a feel for what it'll be like on race day, next week."

He scans our faces to see if anyone has any questions. "Right," he continues. "Pit lane fire precautions."

Dean sits up in his chair.

"If there's a fire in pit lane, we'll sound the klaxons, wave yellow flags, and close the lane. No one moves in pit lane until the firefighters cross over, put the fire out, and give the signal that it's safe to go. All pit crew must wear fire-retardant overalls. If you haven't got them, you'll need to sort this out. You won't be allowed out there without them or decent footwear. No flip-flops."

Again, more chuckles. Flip-flops, really?

"There will be a technical meeting for pit crew later today at three o'clock."

I look over at Mags, who keeps her eyes on Roger, but gives me a nod, so I know she's already on it.

"Right. Your start signals. They'll be given over the klaxon. First one is forty-five minutes before the race and it means that riders can take possession of their machines and start their engines. At thirty minutes, the second signal means stop your engines. At fifteen minutes, you take the bike onto the grid and get yourselves ready to start and restart your engines. At five minutes, put your helmets on and do up your chinstraps, and you should be sorted to go."

The lights come on and Roger introduces us to a guy wearing a bright orange marshal's vest. He shows us the various flags and what they mean: black with an orange disc displaying the rider's number means the competitor stops immediately; yellow is danger, no overtaking and be prepared to stop; white is slow-moving vehicle; and so on.

"If you stop anywhere on the course," Roger says, "we need to know about it so that, one, we can get you back and, two, anyone who's waiting for you also knows where you are. There isn't any touring allowed on the TT course. If you can't proceed at racing speed, stop and get off the road. Riders can come up upon you suddenly, and you'll put them, yourself, the marshals, and spectators in danger."

Roger cups his hands and smacks them together making a loud *pop*. "Look, the way to have a successful run around here is to ride smooth. Don't take risks, build up gradually. Don't come out trying to set the world on fire. We want you to take your time. Your last lap should be your fastest. Approach it sensibly and safely, and you'll go home with a big smile on your face. Enjoy it. It's the best place in the world to ride a bike."

Everyone claps and the electric buzz in the air returns. Mags, Dean, and I go up to Roger, introduce ourselves and chat for a bit.

Roger smiles and shakes our hands. "Guys, how are you doing?"

"We're good," I say. "Listen, thanks again for everything you've done, eh."

"No trouble. So sorry to hear about your dad and Neil."

I nod. "They would have loved to be here."

Roger presses his lips together in a look of condolence, which I appreciate. "If there's anything you need," he says, "you get in touch with me, day or night."

After the meeting, we walk over to the pits where Mags, Dean, and Branna will be during the race. It's a long row of pit stalls, about a hundred, each the width of a closet. We stand inside a pit box. I start repeating what Roger said about how the riders will be coming and going so that Dean gets it, Mags gets it, and I get it too.

"So Branna and I are going to be standing in here?" Dean asks.

I nod and notice he's looking a little pale. "During

race week, this place'll be packed with a few hundred crew, plus technical scrutineers and bikes flying in and out, so watch where you're going. Keep your eyes open to the officials. Do what they say and listen to Mags."

Mags points to the ground. "See that line?"

Dean looks at the white strip running the length of the pits.

"Don't cross it or you'll get clocked by a bike doing just shy of sixty klicks."

He nods. His eyes are big, but he looks serious, like he's recording every word.

"You'll be manually refueling the bike, like Mags taught you," I tell him. "On race day, you'll be loading the fuel tank here." I point up at the standard gravity-fed system above our heads. "The lever to open it is this one. Remember, down is open, to the side is closed. You're going to come at the bike from the side." I get into position and bend my knees, like I'm on the bike.

Mags nudges Dean over to where he needs to stand in relation to where I am. "Don't move out of that two-foot space we talked about," she says to him. "I'll be coming out this way to place the bike on the rear stand. Branna will be out front. She'll remove the gas cap. You will have the gas ready to refuel. Branna will then give Scott his water and clean the windscreen. I'll change his visor. You'll finish refuelling. Branna will replace the gas cap, and I'll take off the rear stand and give Scott a push. Do like we practiced and stay in your space unless Scott or I say so. Got it?"

He nods.

"We've got a tech meeting this afternoon," she continues. "So we'll go over it a few more times. If you have any questions, ask — any time, any place. No question is considered stupid, not when lives depend on it."

I think back to how overloaded I felt when Paul was showing me around the TT course, and I see Dean's eyes darting around, trying to take all this in. I'd be lying if I said he doesn't scare me a little. Dean glances up to where the gas tank would rest. "Are there a lot of fires?"

"It can happen," I answer. "I once saw a guy go down on the track and his fairing caused a spray of sparks that lit up his tank. Instant fireball."

Dean stares at me, and I think I see the penny drop in his head.

"I don't have any fire-resistant overalls," he says.

"I'll get you some," Mags says. "You'll like them. They'll have the TT logo on them."

"Okay, to recap," I say. "During practice week, I'll do two laps, then come in here where you guys will go through the practice pit routine. We probably won't be the only ones going through the motions like this."

"We won't be," Mags confirms.

It's good to know, because it's now hitting me hard just how inexperienced my crew really is. I mean, I have faith in Mags's ability, and Branna's done this before, but I haven't seen them in action yet, just a few mock practices at Alan's place.

We head back to the paddock and Dean pulls a pocket-size magazine from his jacket that says *Supporters Club*. He must have picked it up from the meeting room. "How much is the prize money?" he asks.

Mags snorts. "Dean, you don't ride the TT for the money."

"It depends," I say, "on how many laps you do with the fastest time. The total's probably around twenty grand if you come in first in all six laps."

"What? That's all?"

"Yeah, well, you don't throw yourself at the scenery for cash," I say.

"No kidding," he says.

We blend in with the crowd, passing food concession stands and oversize tents selling souvenirs. Dean, who's had his head down reading the whole time, stops and folds the magazine's spine back on itself so that the page stays open.

"Hey, they have a list in here of the fastest qualifying times from each country." He traces his finger down the column. "The guy from Canada's time was 18:55. You could totally smoke that."

I get a sick feeling in my gut that Dean still doesn't get it.

Early Sunday morning I head into Dean's room. "Hey," I say. "Get up." He moans and keeps sleeping. I have to shake him, hard. "Hey."

He opens one eye. "Dude, where's the fire?" he mumbles.

I pull the covers off him so they fall on the floor. "Come on, shakey-wakey, hands-off snakey. Get dressed. I want to take you out on the circuit on Alan's bike."

He stretches like a cat who's been napping in the sun and knuckle-rubs his eyes. He glances at the bedside clock. "It's four-thirty in the morning, man. What the hey-hey."

"The tourists come out at five. Come on. Get dressed, let's go."

Ten minutes later we're on the TT course.

"You good back there?" I ask.

"Yeah."

"Listen, once the bike's warmed up, I'm going to go pretty fast. If you get freaked out, just tap my shoulder, alright?"

"You know, I've been on a bike before."

"I'm serious, Dean."

"Okay, boss."

I point to a mile-post sign on the road. "I'm roughly five-and-a-half klicks from the start here. Should take me seventy-five seconds to reach this spot during the race." I let him chew on that before I flip down my visor and shift gears. When my tires warm up, gripping more asphalt, and I reach the no-speed-limit sections, I push Alan's bike as hard as it'll let me. We hit speeds of one hundred on the mountain section, which has now officially been changed over from two-way to one-way traffic (it's safer for locals and tourists when everyone's travelling in the same direction). This enables me to use the entire road as a track. From behind us, a white CBR blows past me. A few times Dean tries to stick his head to the side for a look, but then pulls it back because of the wicked-strong headwinds, and I feel him tighten his grip around my waist. When we enter the speed-restricted zone where traffic becomes two-way again, I pull up my visor.

"Holy shit," he yells in a voice that says he's not trying to be funny. "We're still on the *first* lap."

When I take us back to the farm, Dean hops off the bike and removes his helmet.

"Holy cow, man," he says. "You weren't even going all out. Did you see that white CBR fly past us? In that fast section on the mountain, I could actually feel my hands around your waist being pulled apart by the wind." He mimics the action, his eyes practically popping out of his head. "Jesus. My nuts still haven't dropped. You must have legs like tree trunks, 'cause I'd have squished the gas tank with my quads. No wonder Cathy was always freaking out. You have mad skills, man." He stops long enough to look me in the eye and offer a nod of respect. "Balls of chromium steel."

He holds out his hand. I slap mine into it and we shake.

Now I think he gets it.

chapter 12

Monday. I wake up around noon. My heart's pumping like I've been jogging in my sleep. Tonight at five, about a thousand volunteer marshals will be clearing the roads of people, cars, livestock, and debris, like branches and stones. Then it officially becomes the most challenging road circuit in the world. Goosebumps rise all over my body. One guided lap with the travelling marshals, then three more on my own with the big boys.

We spend the day at the paddock. Mags and I check the bike over and over. Maybe we're being a bit obsessive, but you can't have too many eyes on the machinery and it helps pass the time. German Opera dude and Garth are nowhere to be seen, so Dean plays his guitar and sings — mostly to Branna — a Crosby, Stills and Nash song called "Lady of the Island." Man, he must have listened to every record in my dad's collection. You'd think it would bother me that Dean's distracted, but it's actually a good thing, as it keeps them both out of my hair. I'm feeling excited and anxious, like I've downed ten cups of coffee. I miss the way my dad, Neil, and I would crack jokes or how Terry would slap us twice on the back and say, "Go get 'em!" before we headed out. We don't have a routine like that yet and it sucks. I recheck my gear bag: helmet with racing number 86 on it, helmet bag, gloves, boots, body armour, water bottle, cell phone, fistful of earplugs, dog tags with name and blood type on them in case I crash and have to be flown to Noble's hospital.

After lunch, we walk through the riders' restricted area and review the game plan: at five o'clock, Mags will take the bike to the technical station, where it'll pass inspection. Then she'll move it to the warm-up area, plug in the generator, and wrap the tires in tire warmers. She'll wait with Dean and Branna, keep an ear out for the klaxon signals, and wait for me.

When we agree we've got it, I head back to the paddock. Dean and Branna go for ice cream, and Mags strikes up a conversation with Arnie, the mechanic she met yesterday in the technical meeting. I think that if she plays her cards right, maybe she'll score a free lunch from one of the top teams. I chuckle, thinking maybe if I'm lucky, she'll bring a doggie bag back with her. I try to lie down in the van on a blow-up mattress for a nap, but who the hell am I kidding? I can't sleep.

By mid-afternoon, the place is buzzing with hard-core fans who've taken two weeks off for the TT Races. Race week is going to be jam-packed, but this week — practice week — there's still room to move around the paddocks. Fans leisurely wander by, snapping pictures and collecting autographs from the superstars. A few people even make it to the very last row of Paddock C. They all stop, check the number on my bike, flip through the program to see where I'm from, then take a good look at me like they've never seen a Canadian before. A reporter even drops by. I can tell, because reporters have to wear huge, white bibs with large numbers on them so they can be identified from far away. This guy's number is 167.

"You're Scott Saunders from Canada?" he asks with an Irish accent before looking up from his program.

"Yeah," I say.

"I've got a friend in Canada, in Toronto — Stephen G. Miller — do you know him?"

I smile. "No, can't say that I do."

"Mind if I get a few pictures?"

I shrug and look over at Mags, Dean, and Branna, who also shrug.

He readies his camera. "Alright, just keep doing what you're doing and act like I'm not here."

I'm okay with it, but when he starts snapping, it's like my crew's forgotten how to look natural — even Branna. Did Dean just puff out his chest? What a poser. I'm so going to razz him for that later.

Number 167 asks us to spell our names.

"Mind me asking how old you lot are?"

"Dean's eighteen, Branna's twenty, and Mags and I are twenty-two."

He raises his eyebrows, then takes one last photo before thanking us and moving on. I look at my watch. It's quarter to four.

"Mags," I say.

"I'm on it," she replies like she's reading my mind. Mags turns to Dean and Branna. "Let's take the bike to inspection."

My gut does a backflip. Time to get down to business.

Every time my thoughts turn to what I'm about to do — ride the TT — I have to pee. When I was a kid, my dad told me that some riders get so nervous at the startline they piss in their leathers, I laughed like it was the funniest thing I'd ever heard. I ain't laughing now. This is my fourth trip to the can and I still have an hour to go. No matter how many times I rode around the course last week, my paddock neighbour Garth tells me that it'll suddenly be unrecognizable when I hit it at racing speeds. He says it's like the difference between learning on a flight simulator and flying a real plane.

Once my bike passes technical inspection, Mags, Branna, and Dean will set up in the warm-up area and wait for the first klaxon signal so Mags can start the engine.

I collect my inspected gear and helmet from the riders' scrutineering tent and get a couple of "good lucks" from the guys working there. I pass by Karl, who's suiting up in plain view for the world to see. Garth across from me is inside his tent because I can hear him talking to his wife, Jean. I sit on the van's back bumper and stretch my quads, delts, and tri's a little. I didn't do my five-klick run today so on top of the nerves, I'm wound up.

The klaxon blasts over the PA. First signal. My gut goes airborne. Forty-five minutes to go. The bike will be in the warm-up area wrapped in tire warmers. Mags should have it started and will be revving the engine. I head for the porta-potty to pee (again) and do the other number. I come back, hop into the van, and change into my blue undershirt, socks, and gitch. Can't race without wearing all blue. Hey, some people talk to fairies; this is my thing.

I breathe deeply and take my time putting on my leathers, adjusting the knee pads, elbow pads, and back protector, seeking out any tension and releasing it. I make fast fists with my hands and try to clear my mind.

When the second klaxon blares overhead, signalling the thirty-minute mark, my gut does a triple gainer. All bike engines will be cut. I pick up my iPod, then set it down again. I don't need pumping up. My heart's already working overtime.

I slip my bright orange newcomer's vest over my leathers and tape it down so it won't flap around once I hit speeds of up to 180 klicks on public roads through towns and villages. My god. I'm actually going to do this!

Before slipping on my helmet I look up at the sky.

Do 'em proud, I think.

I start to make my way through the paddocks and get lots of pats on the back and handshakes from strangers who've travelled here from all over the world. When I pass by the race chaplain, he touches my arm.

"May God be with you," he says.

"Thanks, Father."

I enter through the restricted gate, pass by the inspection station, and head over to the warm-up area. More nods of the head, slaps on the back, and officials wishing me "a good one." I'm glad I have my visor down because I'm sure my eyes are friggin' huge, pupils blown wide open.

Fifteen minutes to go. Heart's pounding like it's going to burst through my ribs and fly down the track ahead of me. Sixty kilometres of open road at racing speeds. My knees shake a little and my bladder and bowels want to open, again. I want things to get started — now. Let's go already.

I make a pit stop at the porta-potty. Again. Some photographer snaps a photo of me coming out when I'm done — what a tool.

Okay, up the small slope and over to the *parc fermé* (closed park), the area for warming up the machines. I see bikes everywhere in bright, glossy colours. It's like a candy factory's exploded. When the third klaxon sounds, the place comes alive in a rumble of engines firing in a nonstop chorus of short clips and long whines. It sounds like wasps, bees, and hornets. It's like ten thousand cats screaming.

And I've got a gut full of butterflies.

Dean and Branna cluster around Mags and watch her rev the engine. Dad once said that picking out your bike's rev from the pack is like hearing from an old lover. That makes me smile.

"How you doing, Scott?" Mags shouts.

Like I want to puke.

"Good," I holler back. I swing my leg over the seat and slide down into the vinyl groove and this out-of-body sensation hits me, catapulting me out of my skin so it's like I'm watching myself from two feet back. I have to tell myself to breathe as I climb my way back into my body.

Dean keeps his squeal-hole shut for once. In fact, he can barely look at me. He tries to smile, but his eyes betray him. I think he's actually scared for me. I had no idea he cared. Branna holds out my water bottle, and I take it from her and thread the straw between my helmet and chin to take a good pull before passing it back.

The five-minute board lights up. Time to get my race head on. Earplugs in, chinstrap pulled snug. I do some final checks: steering damper, temperature gauge, short squeeze of the brakes. I bounce up and down a little, checking the suspension.

I review the plan: one guided with the travelling marshals, or TMs and another one with some of the fastest guys in the world. Sure, they'll be fitting in four, even five laps, but *they* know the course.

I glide the bike slowly toward the holding pen with all the other orange-vested newcomers. Mags walks beside me. Dean and Branna are gone. Time to silence the noise, the crowds, the cameras. Everything sharpens and clears. Mags slaps me twice on the back. Nice.

The Startline Controller, a blonde woman in overalls, ball cap, and ponytail, talks to all twelve of us one by one. She points to the matrix board.

"Sun spots at Crosby Straight," she shouts over the noise. I nod looking straight ahead, down Glencrutchery Road, like the opening shot of the TT video game. My breathing's shallow and hard, almost rough. My ears fill with the thumping noise coming from my chest. I draw in a long, deep breath through my nose and force my ribs to spread to hold more oxygen. Then I slowly exhale out of my mouth to try to slow things down. Four TMs in front of me, including Roger, wear neon-green vests with capital *M*s on the back. An official comes over and splits us up into groups of three. I'm in the first group.

I get ready and wait for the signal.

First practice: this is it.

chapter 13

The TM takes off, and two other newcomers and I follow. I downshift, then kick it into high gear down Glencrutchery Road, whip past Noble's Park onto a slight left-hander at St. Ninian's — *he's right, it's like flying off the top of the world* — then down Bray Hill, hit 120 in a matter of seconds. Adrenalin floods my system as I drift 'er to the left now, within a foot of the curb for the right-hand sweep, then straight into a dip — *total gut flip, no time to enjoy the G-forces coming out of that* — over to the left now, skim the stone hedge, pass the scrum of photographers catching airtime. The road narrows, and the TM keeps to the left toward Quarter Bridge Pub. Brakes. Downshifts through a tricky right-hander — *good, not bad* — smooth, then straight. Tuck in behind the fairing, but not for long, gear down for Braddan Bridge.

Awkward S-bend, left, followed by a right, then in behind the fairing again — *tuck head, legs, curl toes in, wring the throttle.* Needle climbs on the tachometer, up ahead, a fast right-hander coming into Union Mills, then left into the village, a right, then another left. Cross the bridge to another right rising up, past the post office that used to be home to the Bee Gees — *easy clipping these corners, keep 'er on through here* — fly by the twisted chimneys. Flat out in sixth gear up the hill toward Glen Vine, long right into Ballagarey still in sixth gear, for a long straight — *finally, a breath* — and a fast left into Crosby, crank the throttle through the village — *road's narrower* — pass the Crosby Pub. I keep my head down for the "flying run" on the downhill stretch — *sweet, nice one* — TM guides us through a tricky left-and-right bend at Greeba Castle. Deceptively fast. I keep a fast line, pull left on the bend, maximize speed on the mile-long run toward the sharp right-hander at Ballacraine — *ha, ha, some kid's covering his ears.* Gear down for the ninety-degree-er, shut off, glide through — *good* — about twelve kilometres from the start. Accelerate. Sharp climb to Ballaspur, another left-hander, course drops away at eighty. Tires fight for grip, hurtle downhill toward Ballig Bridge, followed by a blind left-hander — *whoa, that's not my fav* — into a short straight. Squeeze the brake and change gears smoothly — *not bad, not great, good enough*. Enter Laurel Bank with a tricky right-hander, then another right, over to Glen Helen — *quarter-mile mark …*

Things Paul said keep popping into my head:

"Watch the front wheel past the Highway Board 'cause it'll go airborne just before dropping into fifth gear for the right."

"Get your braking right for Ramsey, come in slow."

"Get the apex right at the Verandah and you can drift the bike through the next three corners."

A lot of it I forget. So much to watch for — houses, telephone poles, curbs, manhole covers. Garth's right. It's a completely different course when you're going full out.

I lean my bike to the right and trust the TM's lines. I see why newcomers ride in the middle of the road right on top of the white median line the whole way around — this is scary shit, but it's also *amazing*.

I barrel through the grandstand doing 148 mph. Too fast to spot my team.

On the second lap they let the rest of the riders join us and the TMs leave the course — the training wheels are gone. I tail an experienced rider with clean lines so I can push it a bit just like Paul advised. But it doesn't last because he streaks ahead of me and I feel the bike judder as I brush the edge of his slipstream.

Just past Ramsey into the corner, I gear down to

second instead of first and I come into it way too hard, which throws me off the apex. My back wheel slews left as I rocket around the curve and then the tires catch a grip again. This shakes me. It happens so fast I hardly have time to register it. I go blank on what's coming up next and it takes a while to get back my lines.

It feels like everyone's smoking by me, left, right, and centre. It's like I'm riding a moped. Frigging *amateur.*

Before I know it, my first untimed practice is over and I'm pulling into the warm-up area. Mags, Dean, and Branna come running over. I pull off my helmet and rivulets of sweat run down the sides of my face. In the background, the big boys roar past the grandstand on the last of their laps and all the sidecar racers — a tag team of passenger and driver who both steer the three-wheeled bikes — are warming their engines to get ready for their first time out.

"So? So?" Mags says, desperate to know how it went.

Words. I know some, but I left them somewhere out on the course. All I know is that I have to qualify for next week's race. A flicker of a smile quickly morphs into a big, no, *huge* grin. I start talking a mile a minute.

"That should be illegal. Man, flying down Bray Hill, then the thing … and the airtime at Ballaugh Bridge. Back tire does a little …" My hand takes over, waving like a fish's tail. "Then it's like, light, dark, light, dark with the shadows under the trees at ..." my mind goes blank on where "... it's the place with the thing. And Kirk Michael? Holy shit. It's 170 klicks flat out in sixth gear, and with the buildings, like right there on either side of me, it's like I'm going ten times faster." A cocktail of endorphins and exhaustion washes over me. I feel tired and wired, like I've been out there for three, no *ten* hours. In my brain, the laps merge into one. More babble pours out. I know none of it makes any sense and in a way it's pretty awesome. How can you possibly describe the rush? It's ten times better than sex. I wish I could throw my crew inside my skull so they could feel what I'm feeling.

Branna laughs. "Dean said he had to change his pants the first time you went by."

Dean slaps me on the shoulder. "Dude, that was insane." Then he yanks his hand away and looks at his palm. It's covered in little dead flies, or what they call midges over here. "Ah, that's gross."

I get off the bike and Mags pushes it alongside me as we head back through the crowds toward the paddock. Between all the congratulations from fans and officials, and after I collect my thoughts again, I start telling her all about how the bike handled.

We pass Arnie, who stands with this crew of mechanics, chatting. When he sees us, he smiles.

"You did well," he says.

"Thanks," both Mags and I say. I put a hand on her shoulder and give it a squeeze.

chapter 14

Tuesday. Time trials. This is the second day of practice, but the difference is that today they start timing my laps, and my crew practices their first pit stop. In order to qualify for next week's race, I have to come within 115 percent of the third-fastest rider's lap time. If my time isn't fast enough today, then I have three more days to try again. Twelve laps to get it right. If I don't, I don't race. If I blow an engine, I don't race. The thought of not making it to next week's Supersport 600 race makes me twitch, so I try to put it out of my mind. Last night, Mags and I stayed up late, making adjustments to the bike. It wobbled and the damping was off. I had to head inside the house at around one in the morning to get some sleep, while Mags kept working on the oil and filter changes.

At our paddock today we pretty much do what we did yesterday: Dean and Branna hang out, I help Mags double-check the bike. Arnie pops by for a chat and to see how it's going and if there is anything he can do. It's kinda nice that he's going out of his way to look in on us. I found out yesterday that this is his twenty-third time at the TT.

Two members of the press show up. One's holding a notepad and the other has a camera with him. It doesn't take long to figure out why they're so interested in us and it isn't because we're the good-looking Canadians. We're a team of four, two guys and two girls, ranging in age from eighteen to twenty-two. Apparently it's newsworthy.

"How'd it feel riding the TT course for the first time, Scott?" he asks.

"Incredible," I say. "Nothing can prepare you for this. There's so much to take in. With every lap I'm learning my way around more and more."

He turns to Mags. "So you're the chief mechanic?"

I can't tell from his accent if he sounds condescending or not. Arnie also gives me a look as if he's wondering the same thing.

"Yes," she answers, wiping her hands on her tool rag.

"Have you worked only on modified street bikes or full-on race bikes?"

She doesn't blink. "Both."

He takes a good look at my race bike. "So you've ported the head on the bike?"

Mags crosses her arms. "Altered the timing and the duration but not the lift. That's not legal in his race class. It's got to remain homologated."

Arnie and I smirk. *Ha. Busted,* I think. *Nice try, Mr. Reporter.*

"If that's all —" Mags has taken her measure of him and now, bored, she flicks her gaze away "— I have to get back to work." The photographer snaps one more picture as she goes over the checklist again.

The press draws a crowd of people who gawk, and with all of us being confined to a ten-by-ten canopy pop-up tent, we feel like zoo animals. People mutter to each other as they flip through the race guide trying to figure who number 86 is.

A little kid in a TT sweatshirt is nudged forward by his dad to ask for my autograph. I smile because I remember being that kid. I sign his race guide by my name. From the corner of my eye, I see Dean smirking. I can tell he's dying to say something, but he's doing his best to restrain himself.

When the crowd shuffles along, making their way back to the more glamorous race tents, Dean saunters over and pitches his voice real high. "Oh, Mister Saunders, will you sign my ass cheek?" He then drops his drawers partway and wiggles his rear end. I laugh and make like I'm going to give it a swift kick.

Washroom: check. Helmet: check. Leathers: check. Gloves: check. Boots: check. Earplugs: check. Dog tags: check. Cell phone: check. Yeah, a cell phone, because who knows where on the course you might need to stop and make a call.

In the van I change into my leathers and get into the race zone when a loud *thwap* on the sliding door startles the hell out of me.

"Scott!" Dean shouts and I hear panic in his voice. "Where're the safety-wire pliers? Mags needs them and the hose clamp."

I hop out of the van. His hollering wakes Garth's and Jean's baby in the tent across from us and she starts wailing.

"What's going on?" I say and head for the toolbox. I start fishing through it — damn, the guy should know his tools by now, enough to get this himself and not come barging in like a wild boar. "What did the tech inspectors say?"

"I dunno, Mags just told me to go run and ask you."

Go run? I find the safety-wire pliers and the hose clamp and give them to him. He takes off.

I'm too psyched to let this go now. What does she need the pliers for? Did she forget to safety-wire the oil filter? She'll need my help if she did because she'll have to pull the lower fairing off. I finish suiting up, grab my gear and helmet, and head for the inspection station. Hauling ass in full leathers, weaving through a crowd is like how it looks — slow and uncomfortable.

The first klaxon blares overhead. Forty-five minutes until the first official timed practice. I break out in a light sweat, which sucks because when you're hitting high speeds, the sweat turns cold. Mags should have passed technical inspection a half-hour ago and already been in the *parc fermé.* I try not to jump to conclusions about what might be wrong with the bike. It's wasted energy and I could psych myself out, making a mountain out of a mole hill. Two officials part the orange plastic fence bordering the tech area from the fans and the riders to let me and Dean through. I spot Mags crouched down by the bike. Her eyes flick up at me, then away, fast.

"What's going on?"

"It's okay," she says, keeping her head down. "I got it."

I watch her hands, and her movements are choppy, shaky.

"Is it the safety wire?"

"It's okay," she repeats. "Don't worry about it."

What the hell's with the attitude?

"I forgot to safety-wire the oil filter. Alright? No big deal. I'm fixing it."

But it *is* a big deal because this isn't the Scott show or the Mags show. We're supposed to be a team. I look at Dean, who shrugs. Useless twit.

"Dean," she says. "Get me more safety wire. Do you know what that is?"

I pray that he does.

"No."

"Oh my god," I say and a technician looks our way.

Mags takes off running. She exits through the orange barrier and darts into the crowd.

Because we're the last of the solo bikes to be scrutinized, sidecar riders are now queuing and waiting for us to get a move on. If we don't hurry up, we could run out of time and miss our chance at tonight's practice. I suddenly feel like I've gone deaf to hearing everything but the heavy pounding in my chest. I need all the practice laps I can get to qualify. "Why didn't she bring the bike here an hour ago?" I ask.

Dean shrugs. Again, twit.

"I dunno. She was talking with that Arnie guy."

I breathe in some patience. "Where's Branna?"

"Waiting in our pit."

"Well, at least *one* of you is ready."

People behind the orange fence part to make way for more sidecar drivers and their bikes to come through. Each minute she's gone is one minute less my machine could be with all the others. One of the bike inspectors shoots me a look of concern. I tell myself to chill, that it'll all be okay, but it doesn't work. I keep thinking: tonight they start timing my laps for the qualifiers. I *need* to be out there.

Mags squeezes through the orange barrier, runs over, and crouches down by the bike. She says nothing and doesn't look at me. As she loosens a bolt, the cut end of the lock wire slices her knuckle and a thin blood-filled line rises on her skin.

"Step back," I tell her. "You're doing it wrong."

She looks at me, her eyes flashing with anger. "How about you don't tell me how to fix the friggin' bike and I won't tell you how to friggin' ride!"

I think I nearly fall down. I've never heard language like that from her before. I step back, to show I'm not looking for a fight, but watch her closely. I'm not riding if I get even the slightest feeling that she's doing a sloppy job.

The second klaxon sounds. A half-hour to go. It's also

the end of warm-up. I'll be riding my bike cold … that's if I get to ride at all.

"Dean, get the scrutineer," she tells him. So what does the guy do? He whistles and snaps his fingers like he's ordering a beer in a bar. One of the inspectors, who looks like a crusty old salt, glances at us, not amused. Jesus, that's all we need, a pissed-off inspector. He comes over, crouches down to get in real close with a critical stare. He touches a few things, checks over her work. I don't take my eyes off Mags. I know she can see me in her peripheral vision, but she won't acknowledge my gaze. The inspector nods and puts a small sticker on the machine to show that it's passed muster. I exhale and Mags hauls the bike off its stand and starts pushing it through the chaotic mob of officials, racers, mechanics, and press toward the warm-up area. She looks behind her at the bike stand and tools on the ground. "Dean," she shouts, "pick them up and let's go!" He scrambles for the pieces and runs to catch up with her. Some of the sidecar drivers watching us laugh.

As Mags makes her way up the slope a photographer runs ahead so he can snap photos of a five-foot-nothing, twenty-two-year-old woman pushing a four-hundred-pound racing bike. To avoid a sudden collision she has to tip the bike dangerously to one side. She recovers, but not before it's captured on film. She should have plowed the guy over. I so want to confront him and get in his face, but I've got my own problems. I stop to take a leak. Yeah, my bike's cold. Yeah, the practice laps are now being timed. Yeah, I need just one of those laps to qualify. Okay, so my first lap's a write-off because the bike isn't fully warmed-up. It's not the end of the world. Fine. On the second lap I'll give 'er. Problem solved.

Final klaxon sounds. Mags revs the engine like she's trying to make up for lost time. Neither of us looks happy. No time to get into it now. Gotta focus.

They just better have their shit together for refuelling.

My first and second laps go pretty well, considering the drama with scrutineering. I roll up the return road and head back to pit lane. Mags places the bike on the rear stand and I relax and drop my legs, giving them a stretch. Branna removes the gas cap and Dean slips the funnel into the opening and starts refueling. Mags tears off my visor. Branna hands me my drink. I take a swig and the water's so icy cold my throat tightens up. Is she trying to break my teeth? I have to fight through the pain to suck back enough liquid to stay hydrated. Mags is spending way too much time replacing my visor. It's not snapping into place. I toss my water bottle into the closet-size pit box so I can take over. I snap on the visor. She hadn't used enough pressure. More practice. Branna cleans the windscreen as Mags goes around back, ready to remove the rear stand. I watch Dean. His hands shake. He lifts the gas tube out, and when Branna goes to replace the cap, their timing is off and hands collide, sending the cap careening down the side of the bike and in behind the fairing.

Shit. "Mags," I holler, and get off the bike.

"What?" she says coming around the front.

"Gas cap's behind the fairing. Help me lift the bike." She pulls Dean back and out of our way and together we tip up the bike. The cap rattles its way through and I also hear the rapid-fire *click-click-click-click* of a camera. Gas spills out of the tank as the cap hits the ground. I get on the bike as Mags replaces the cap. I grab the rag from Branna's hand and mop up the excess gas. I start up the bike and Mags gives me a push.

I head back out to the starters' area and wait for instructions from officials so I can get in another practice lap.

Well, that was shit, I think.

I take off down Glencrutchery Road and get halfway down Bray Hill when my visor gets pelted by half-a-dozen midges, all right in the same spot, creating a big smudge between my eyes. I reach for the first of my two tear-offs to get rid of the bugs. So much for rationing, I've got two more laps, nearly seventy-five miles to go.

Third lap: quarter-mile mark, roughly five or six miles from the start — watch for wet patches under trees, onto a second left, lean to the right for Sarah's Cottage — *the place where Dean thought a hot chick lived.* Up to Creg Willey's Hill, tenth-mile marker, for a tight right-hander, followed by a left, taking me to Cronk-y-Voddy straight — *the "fun" stretch* — doing 120. Tons of body-pounding airtime, come out of it and straight into a double right-hander. Drop down for the left-hand bend and past the eleventh milestone, and there's Handley's and the chicane. Sweet, fast straight, a perfect line. Over two bridges coming up on Barregarrow. Top right-hand bend, sweep down to a tight, low left-hand corner at the thirteenth milestone, back up to 120. Fairing scrapes the ground, straighten 'er up, drift 'er into Kirk Michael, narrow, whitewashed village — *claustrophobic, like racing down an alleyway.* Clip the curbstone, ride wall to wall to wall — *make that mother strip straighten out* — gear up for Birkin's Bend. Fast right-hander, then a quick left-hand sweep onto a fast straight leading to the humpback bridge, up, out, negotiate the awkward right- and left-hand corners out of the village. Full bore along the snaky road, past the zoo — *hello, Mr. Otter billboard* — to Quarry Bends, a right, left, right, left, pass the halfway post, hit Sulby Straight, fifth gear coming out the left-hander. Max the throttle, head down, straight road ahead. Narrow toward the horizon. Hold that throttle open, 131, 148, 157, 168 mph. Sulby Village, lean over slightly, pass Ginger Hall Hotel, then a left-hander over the hill, down to the left- and right-hand bends of Kerroomooar. Keep left, to Glen Tramman. Spot tree with a massive "K" painted on it, keep to its right — *like Paul said* — on the straight to Milntown Cottage. Watch for curb jutting into the road above the rise. Enter Ramsey — *halfway mark* —

Garth told me that the best way to remember the next bend is to watch for the top of a fence post that is painted white. There are a lot of hidden markers like this around the course. You just need to know how to spot them, and I need all the help I can get.

After practice, we check my time results on the big screen outside the race office. The third-fastest lap of the night ends up being 18:08, which means that I needed a new time of 20:51 to qualify for next week's race.

I don't even come close. I feel drained, exhausted, and cranky like my blood sugar's out of whack.

We head back to the paddock, looking like one sorry-ass team. I rip off my gloves and toss them to the ground.

"Branna: water's too cold. Can't drink it when it's icy." I pick up a pair of pliers. "Dean, these are safety-wire pliers." I toss them down onto some wires. "And that's safety wire. I don't even want to talk about the gas cap." I look at Mags, think about the lousy exchange we had at scrutineering and my patience runs thin. "If you're going to send him to get something, make sure he knows what it is. And take the bike for inspection earlier."

She folds her arms across her chest and says nothing.

"And when I ask what's wrong, you need to tell me," I add.

"It was no big deal. I fixed it," she says.

Who is this person? I think. "I don't care. If I ask, it means I need to know. I'm not your parents, so don't blow me off like I am. Everyone screws up, but when you don't talk about it, I can't trust you, and I'm not racing if I don't feel safe."

She presses her lips together making a tight, thin line. "Fine."

chapter 15

Wednesday. I sort of slept. It was more like my mind ran all night with the occasional five-minute blackout. Three more days to get my ass qualified. In the paddock, we start working as a team. A frosty, cold-vibed team, but a team. You'd have thought we were army grunts by everyone's clipped speech.

"Fuel loaded?" Mags demands.

Dean picks up the wheelbarrow with the tanks in them. "Yup."

"Pit board?" Mags says.

"Yup."

Mags turns to Branna. "Tire warmers?"

"Yeah."

"Air pig?"

"Yeah."

Mags and I barely talk to each other at all. We do what we have to do on the bike, then go our separate ways.

She turns to Dean. "Compressor?"

"Yeah."

Dean's been real quiet. He's been keeping out of my way, which is smart.

Mags turns to me. "You good?"

"Yup."

"Okay, let's do this."

I'm at the back of the pack in the holding pen with the rest of the riders, slowly making my way to the start-line as the bikes take off, one every ten seconds. I try to breathe and relax. Tension creeps across my neck like a tarantula. When it's my turn, the Start Controller tells me about wet patches at Glen Helen, then gives me the tap on the shoulder and I'm off — for about ten feet because I feathered the damn clutch and choked. *Shit.* A total noob mistake. Last time I did this I was sixteen years old. One of the top guys flies past me going 175 mph on his second lap and I feel the wind resistance give me a good push, jarring me a little. No time to wallow in my asinine stupidity, so I put my bike in gear and go. I race by the grandstand, then Noble's Park and head through the Gates of Hell. All the way around the island on my first lap it's like the bike wants to do one thing and I want it to do something else. I'm knocked around like a hockey puck in the playoffs. I'm bouncing from gutter to manhole cover and I'm even managing a tank slapper on the approach to Glentramman. My body tightens like a vice grip from throat to nuts. It's like I'm riding a totally different course. It's like I'm riding Dean's motocross bike, minus the shocks, and getting personal with every bump and dip. I loathe the stretch around Creg ny Baa where the road surface is like shell-grip — bumpy as hell — I swear I can even smell it.

Let this practice run be good enough to qualify.

After my second lap, I pull in for refuelling.

Branna feeds a straw up between my chin and helmet. I take it from her and drink. The water is cool, not icy. My visor snaps off and is replaced quickly, smoothly. The windshield is scrubbed and made smudge-free. We're making great time, working with precision, like a well-oiled machine. Maybe I should say something like "Keep it up and we'll be ready for next week's race." Then I think, no. One good pit stop doesn't make up for yesterday's mistakes. Best to keep them on their toes. Besides,

I haven't qualified yet. So I don't get anyone's hopes up.

Mags takes the bike off the rear stand as Dean steps back with the empty fuel container. Branna screws the gas cap back on. Mags pushes me to get started and I'm out of there. Nice.

On my final lap, past the halfway point and coming up to Sulby Straight, I'm feeling good again, like this time's a total keeper. I even get a chance to tail one of the better riders. I think I might have even qualified. I'm about ready to take 'er up to 180 mph when I see a marshal waving the black flag. I squint to see the racer's number on the chalkboard they hold out by the side of the road. In big numbers it says "86." That's me. No way. What for? When I start to slow down, I can smell why. Burning oil. Marshals must have spotted it a few clicks back and radioed ahead. I pull off the road and get as close to the stone wall as I can. The marshal across the road points to where I should park my bike so it's off the course. About ten feet farther up there's a small entranceway to a field fenced off by a swinging gate. Two bikes go flying by.

"You alright then?" A guy in a bright orange vest shouts from across the road because he, too, is restricted from crossing.

I nod and wave, but say nothing. Too much adrenalin

coursing through me and I'm bummed that I'm out when I was doing amazing. I walk my bike up to where the marshal said I should go. I lean it carefully against a fence post. Then I open the gate to enter the field and shut it behind me. Sheep scatter. Frig, this sucks. I pace for a bit to calm down, then head back through the gate. I crouch down next to my bike to see what the problem is and feel the leathers pinch the back of my knees. I straighten up. I tell myself to let it go, that I can't do anything about it. Shit happens. Settle down. Breathe.

Two more riders fly by. They're so close I could put my hand out and touch them. I reach for my inside pocket to grab my cell phone so I can call the team and let them know I'm okay, but there's nothing there.

"Bullocks. Shit. Shite!" I holler. I left the damn phone plugged in to recharge in the van. Frig, they're going to kill me.

"Hey!" I shout to the bald marshal when there are no bikes racing by. "I don't have my phone. I need you to contact my crew and let them know I'm here."

A succession of bikes fly past before we can talk again. "I haven't got a phone," he says. "But race control knows you're here." He holds up his TETRA radio.

I rip off a string of swear words, then park my ass on the ground. There's nothing I can do now. Let's hope

Mags listened during the technical meeting about riders missing in action and she checks with race control for updates. They'll say something like "Rider X stopped at Y and requires pickup." We should have practiced for that.

I do a rough time-count in my head. I got pulled off and have been dicking around in the field for what, five minutes? And who knows how long it'll take before they get the message — another five? They'll be expecting me at the grandstand soon. How could I forget my phone? I thought I did all the checks. I'm a moron.

I guess it's nothing but hurry-up-and-wait now. Wait until the riders finish, then the sidecar practice, and then the okay for the roads to reopen. Meanwhile Mags, Dean, and Branna will have to haul the equipment back to the paddock, pack up the van and come find me.

An hour and thirty minutes pass before the travelling marshal rides by, indicating that time trials are over and the roads will soon open. Five minutes after that and it's like every Manx citizen and TT fan is on the road, going home or riding the course. Total chaos. People honk their horns and wave as they pass me. Some slow down and ask if I need a lift and I plaster on a stupid grin and say, "No thanks." One guy tosses me a bottle of water, which I appreciate.

"Sorry it ain't a pint," he shouts.

Me too, I think.

Finally I see Alan's van. I scissor my arms and Branna flashes the headlights. She pulls off to the side as best as she can and traffic slows down to a crawl because we're still half on the narrow road. Bikers start using the centre line, creating a third traffic lane.Vehicles honk, but I don't think they're mad; I think they're just acknowledging the situation.

Mags slides the passenger-side door open, gets out and slams it with such force the van rocks. Then the vehicle's back doors pop open and Dean jumps down. They both look pissed off.

Mags marches up to me, grabs my wrist, twists it so my palm's face up and slaps my cell phone into it. I can practically see the lasers shooting from her eyes.

"Next time take it."

"I'm sorry," I say, but my apology falls on deaf ears. She instructs Dean on how to load up the bike. Since they've got it covered, I leave them and slide into the passenger seat.

I sit there, feeling like a tool. Branna taps the steering wheel to some tune in her head. "You alright? Had us pretty worried."

"On three," Mags says to Dean. "One, two, three."

The van dips as it takes on extra weight. She rolls the bike forward and then clips it into the secured paddock stand before hauling on the tie-downs and compressing the forks. She does the same on the back end.

Dean slides the ramp back into the van and the rear doors shut with a *thwunk, thwunk*. Branna shifts the van into drive and we're out of there.

I clench my teeth for the onslaught.

"You scared the hell out of us," Mags says, her voice stern and even. "We didn't know where you were."

"Yeah," Dean adds. "We thought you kissed the scenery."

From the back seat Mags hauls off and punches me in the arm. "You're always on our case, ragging on us about being prepared, and there you go, doing the worst thing ever."

Dean hits me in the same spot. "Yeah. A helicopter took off when you didn't show, so of course we thought it was going for you, *asshole*."

"Okay, alright," I say, clutching the place where they'd both punched me, "stop riding my ass. I tried to borrow a phone from a marshal, but he didn't have one. I'm sorry, okay? It won't happen again."

"We're going back to the paddock, unloading the bike, then Dean, Branna, and I are going for a stiff drink,"

Mags says. "You can come with, if you want," she all but mumbles.

I ignore her invite; it's clear by her tone they don't want me along.

I shake my head. "You can't," I say. "Bike's leaking oil. That's why they pulled me off."

"Ah, hell." She throws her arms in the air, then slaps them onto her lap. "No. Not tonight; I need a break."

It's like she's just hit me again. "You can't bail whenever you want and get shit-faced," I say. "You said you wanted to mechanic a big race. Breakdowns and all-nighters come with the gig."

She looks at me, caught off guard. "What? That's not what I said —"

"Terry wouldn't blow this off," I say.

Her jaw drops. "Oh, you want to bring Terry into this?" A sharp edge appears in her voice. "Do you want to know why it's so hard for him to see you, Scott?"

I blink, dumbfounded. How the hell would she know anything about my business with Terry?

When she sees the stunned look on my face, she backs off. "Look, Scott. Not everything's about you right now."

What's that supposed to mean? I think.

"Guys," Dean interrupts, "let's be cool. Scott, you have no idea what Mags — what we've all been through tonight." He holds his hands out, palms facing up in Neil's Jesus Christ pose. I just about blow a gasket.

I knock one of his hands away. "You think you've got everyone fooled with your good-boy act, don't you?" I look at Branna. "Has he told you he's got a criminal record?" Her eyes shift from the road to me, her expression registering surprise. "Yeah, breaking and entering," I say. "Even went to juvie for it."

Dean's horrified expression quickly hardens.

"So," I go on, "since no one gives a shit about qualifying, go ahead, drink up, blow off Neil and my dad. I'm the only one taking this seriously anyway."

It's quiet for the rest of the ride, just the sound of the bike forks compressing in the back as we turn corners and hit bumps. Branna pulls into our paddock and parks the van. We all get out, slamming the doors and taking off in different directions. I don't care where they go. I make my way to the grandstand to check the leader-board. Large crowds gather around the top riders' paddocks, slowing me down. I finally make it to the electronic screen and spot my name. Lap time: 20:53. This is my best time so far, and by my calculations, I've qualified. I knew the third lap was a keeper. I slap my fist into my open palm. Mission friggin' accomplished. I get to race next week.

Then the screen goes blank.

"Uh-oh, that can't be good," an official next to me says. He puts his ear to his radio.

"What's going on?" I ask.

"There's been some discrepancy on the lap times," he says. As we wait for more information he starts telling me about one of the riders who ended up coming off at Ballagarey and taking a trip to Noble's hospital. The latest update is that he has a few cracked ribs. Guy's lucky, I think.

The race times come back up.

Yeah, there was a discrepancy alright. The qualifying time has changed because the third-fastest rider's time was entered wrong. My best time misses out by a lousy eighteen seconds.

I still haven't qualified.

chapter 16

It's past midnight and I'm about to remove the engine so I can tear it apart when Mags walks into the garage dressed and ready to work. She leans against the door frame, staring at me, and I'm not sure if she looks mad because I'm working on the bike, or because she has to work all night, or because she has to work with me.

I pick up the hundred-pound engine and she hurries over to clear a space on the workbench so I have somewhere to set it down.

"Thanks," I mumble.

"Did you check the oil filter?" she asks.

"Yeah, it's alright."

She wipes her hands on her rag. "Could be the output shaft seal."

"That's what I was thinking."

I reach for my water bottle and take a swig.

She picks up her tool rag and tosses it across one shoulder. "And just so you know, I'm not drunk. I had one drink and that was a couple of hours ago. I'm all about seeing this through. I just needed five seconds to myself. I don't think asking for a little time out is too much." She picks up a speed handle.

"It's not," I say.

She chucks the handle onto the table and it clatters, startling me. "You know, Scott, what you said to us today was totally uncalled for. We *are* taking this seriously. You don't know how hard Dean's been trying to get things perfect in practice. You should've heard him tearing a strip off himself for screwing up in the pits on Tuesday with the gas cap. The guy respects you. When you're not around, he's right beside me asking questions. He doesn't want to mess it up. He knows how much this means to you, Neil, and your dad. And I've been working day and night making sure everything's right."

Before I can say anything, I see tears leaking out of her eyes. Wait, is she crying? Mechanics don't cry.

Mags looks up at the ceiling as if it'll funnel the water back into her head. "Do you know what —" her voice grows thin and brittle "— do you know what my first thought was when we didn't see you come into the pits?"

I shake my head.

"I thought ..." She taps her chest trying to help dislodge what she wants to say. "What did *I* do to that bike that killed Scott?"

Shivers run through my body. It chokes me up to see her so upset. "Ah, Mags, you didn't do anything."

She wipes her face with her hands, dries them on her overalls, and half-laughs even though she's not trying to make a joke. "Maybe I'm not cut out for this. I was stupid to think I could take this on."

"What? Are you kidding? There's a reason why Terry hired you. You've got skills. I've known the guy all my life and he wouldn't bullshit."

She rolls her eyes like Terry and I are lying. I want to give her a hug and tell her it's okay, or something, but I dunno. Then I think, screw it, and draw her in close, wrapping my arms around her to show her that things are good between us. She hugs me back, tight, then pulls away and wipes her eyes dry.

"I'm sorry," she says.

"Don't be."

"Well, I am."

"Well, I'm sorry for being a jerk."

"You should be." She laughs.

We start working on the engine. She disassembles and

I wipe down the oil and clean the parts. We listen to classic-rock songs on the radio and it makes me a little nostalgic, thinking about my dad and Terry and how we used to work together late into the night like this. To pass time, the two of them would dish out advice on girls and my racing career, or tell stories about travelling across Canada and the U.S. by bike in the late '80s and all the adventures they'd had.

When we work our way to the gearbox, Mags picks up the oil seal. Sure enough, there's a tear in it.

She chucks it into the garbage, then sifts through her spares box for another one.

I run my hand down the length of my face. It's after three in the morning. I should get some rest. I'm about to call it a night when she dumps the parts drawer onto the table. Nuts and ball bearings scatter and roll in all directions. She sifts through the bits, then grabs another drawer and dumps it out. This is the first time I've seen her make a mess.

She pinches her eyes closed with her thumb and finger and it leaves an oil smudge in the crease between her eyes and nose.

"I don't believe this," she says.

"Believe what?"

"I didn't pack a seal."

I look at the parts on the table. "You sure?" I sift through them, spreading them out. Nothing.

"God, how could I have been so stupid?" she says. "It's like one disaster after another. It's a *twenty-five-cent part*."

"Hey," I say in a reassuring voice. "This is a hiccup, not a throw-up. We'll pick one up tomorrow. What time do the bike shops open?"

"Eight-thirty," she says, shaking her head.

"Okay, so we'll head over to the paddock to see if anyone has an extra, and if not, we'll hit the repair shops. Then we'll come back here and finish. Okay?" I offer her my hand to help her up and she takes it and nods.

"Alright. Let's call it a night."

I wake up with that fast-pounding heart-attack feeling and look at the bedside clock. It's nearly noon. I get dressed and race downstairs to find Mags in the kitchen with the phone book splayed open on the table. She glances up at me with red, puffy eyes. I don't think she slept last night. The phone next to her rings and she snatches it from its cradle.

"Hello? … Yes, that's right, I'm the one who called about the output shaft seal."

I watch her drum a red pen against a sheet of paper that has a dozen phone numbers on it and there's a line through every one. The farther down the list, the deeper the scratches.

"Are you serious? How long will that take?" I watch her face. It doesn't look good. "Overnight?" she asks.

My gut drops like I'm flying over Ballaugh Bridge and I can't see the ground under my front wheel. I have to sit down or my knees will give out.

"Well, if that's the best you can do, then yes, please ship it overnight express to arrive first thing tomorrow and I'll come pick it up."

Her fingers take down the Steam Packet delivery details, and then she hangs up. She can't look at me. "Bike's not going to be ready for tonight's practice," she says.

I feel heat rise from my gut and spread across my chest. "Did you try Roger and everyone at the paddock?"

She nods. "Everyone. I even got Manx Radio to make an announcement to see if anyone on the island had a seal. I found one, but it was another rider's only spare and he didn't want to give it up even though I said we'd replace it within twenty-four hours."

I want to yell at the top of my lungs and punch a wall or something, but I clamp my mouth and clench my fists instead. She'll get even more upset and I'll only screw up my driving hand.

She bows her head and her shoulders slump. "I'll let the TT office know we won't be in tonight's practice."

Four more chances to qualify for next week's race, *gone.*

I have to get out of the house — now. I head for the garage and look around for Alan's bike because I need to take off and just ride, lose myself on the road. But it's not there. Then I remember Dean saying he was taking it out to get used to how it handles before riding it in the Ramsey Sprint on Saturday.

I leave the garage, not sure where I'm going or what I'm doing. I stop, take a breath, and consider my options: I could hang around, walk up the road to watch tonight's practice like a fan, but the thought of standing on the sidelines makes me want to throw up. No. I have to get the hell away.

I take Alan's van and drive, taking whatever road leads me away from the TT course. After about twenty minutes I end up at the southernmost tip of the island at a place called the Calf of Man. I get out, slam the door, and zip up my coat against the strong winds. Near the edge of the cliff hundreds of birds that look like seagulls wail and scream as they jut in and out of cliffside perches. Not far out at sea is a lighthouse on a rocky outcrop they call Chicken Rock. I park my butt near the cliff's edge and watch the choppy waves throw themselves onto the jagged boulders surrounding the lighthouse. Somehow I don't think they call the place Chicken Rock because of the poultry.

I draw in a few deep breaths of sea air in an attempt, as my dad used to say, to get my head calibrated.

Why does everything have to suck so much? All I wanted to do was ride in the TT, and ever since I got here, it feels like one colossal mistake after another. I snort and think maybe the trip is cursed. My dad's dead, Neil's dead, and Terry … who the hell knows what's up with him? He won't even give me the time of day. He might as well be gone from my life too. To hell with it, I think. I'm sick and tired of the guy acting like I don't exist. I pull out my cell phone from my pocket. Screw the roaming charges, I want to know why he's being an asshole. I dial his number.

"Hello."

My throat grows tight. Instead of giving him a piece of my mind, I suddenly want to start bawling. "Terry? It's Scott —"

"You've reached Terry's Cycle. Sorry, I can't take your call. Please leave a message aft —"

I hang up and grip the phone hard to prevent it from flying into the sea.

I stand and holler, "Screw you, Terry!" A flock of birds perched along the cliff take off, screaming.

That's it, I think. I'm closing the door on this or it'll just drive me nuts. I vow to put Terry out of my head.

I walk back to the van and decide that from now on, I'm only looking forward, not back. Best-case scenario is that the countershaft seal comes in tomorrow morning, Mags fixes the bike, and I catch tomorrow night's practice. The worst-case scenario is that it gives me one less day to qualify, and if I don't make it for next week's race, I'll go through the rest of my life knowing that I've let my dad, Neil, and everyone else down.

Friday. Last practice. If I don't qualify then it's game over, no Supersport 600 race on Monday. I feel like I'm getting crowded off my own bike. I just gotta ride like I did on Wednesday, but better.

The weather's been lousy all morning, overcast and friggin' cold. We go through our routine and the bike passes inspection. I get dressed and start making my way through the paddocks. Mags calls me to say that there's fog on the mountain, which means unacceptable race conditions because the helicopter can't land if there's an emergency. So the other riders and I retreat to our dens. I lie down in the van. It's more hurry-up-and-wait time.

I tune into Manx Radio for updates, but the repetitive commercials about ensuring that all livestock are secured drives me nuts, so I shut it off. Every fifteen minutes I call Mags on the cell and ask for updates.

"Still foggy on the mountain stretch," she says. "Delayed another half-hour."

"Okay, call me in twenty." I lie back down, resting the phone on my chest, and put on my iPod.

Fifteen minutes later, I get a call, but I already know what she's going to say. I can hear the rain on the van's roof. Frig. Any more delays and there won't be a practice run today. In the next hour I manage to catch a nap and wake up five minutes before Mags calls. Finally some good news. My heart jumpstarts and the other riders and I emerge like groundhogs in February, checking to see if there're six more weeks of waiting. The crowd in wet raincoats parts to let me, Garth, Karl, and the others through the now-soaked paddock, our feet squashing through muddy ground. We head over to the restricted gate and up the slope where nearly a hundred motorcycles worth a few million dollars have been sitting all this time in the rain, waiting for their riders to claim them.

I see Dean and Branna. We exchange nods. Mags

chats with Arnie and when I get closer he nods a hi to me and tells me to have "a good one," then waves goodbye to Mags and leaves.

"How you doing?" she asks.

I hold up a shaky hand. "Like a rock," I say and chuckle.

"Got your phone?"

"Yup, but I won't need it." Mags squeezes my shoulder.

There's an announcement over the PA. The practice session will begin in fifteen. Mags and the other mechanics begin firing up the bikes and Dean wipes the rainwater off my seat with the sleeve of his sweater.

In less than two minutes what was once a quiet, practically deserted warm-up area is now a horde of riders, fans, mechanics, press, and sponsorship bigwigs. It's like someone's just cranked a master dial for tension and excitement from zero to eleven. One hundred engines roar to life and it smells like wet tar, exhaust, garages, and motorcycle racing. Mags walks the bike alongside me as officials tell us to assemble in order by number. We join the queue at the back.

I sit on my bike and photographer 167 takes our picture. I block him out and focus on getting into the zone. Breathe. Qualify. Do this for Dad and Neil.

More waiting. Another five minutes goes by. If we

don't hurry up, I'll have to take a whiz again. Up ahead, near the front of the line, one of the top riders gets off his bike, followed by two more.

"I'll go find out what's happening," Mags says and jogs over to Arnie and his crew, who have all the radio equipment. I flick up my visor. I already know what he's going to say because I hear engines being cut.

Up ahead, a slick-looking TV journalist interviews one of the riders, who shrugs into the camera and says, "Well, it's just the Isle of Man, isn't it? I mean, we're out in the middle of the sea. You're bound to get weather like this, aren't you? Just the way it is."

Mags jogs back. "Like fog soup on the mountain stretch. They're cancelling practice and reworking the schedule. Make-up day is Sunday."

I loosen my chinstrap. God, I think, then sigh. One more day.

The sky starts spitting again and crew members from all over come running, holding out huge umbrellas for their riders. Mags takes the bike back to the paddock and Dean wanders over in my direction. The hood of his sweater is up and his hands are shoved into his pockets.

"This sucks, eh?" he says.

I inhale, then exhale hard, letting my cheeks puff out. "It's like this is never going to friggin' happen."

"Yeah," he says. "I wouldn't worry though. You'll get 'em on Sunday."

I shake my head and remove my gloves. "I dunno, man. This is one of the hardest and most draining things I've ever done in my life."

Dean slaps me on the shoulder. "Dude, if anyone can do this, it's you."

I wonder why he's being supportive all of a sudden, especially after I outed him in front of Branna.

We walk down the hill toward the restricted gates. "Look," I say. "I'm sorry for spazzing out on you guys in the van."

He laughs even though he's not trying to be funny. "Yeah, you were asshole-supreme."

"I'm just trying to do the best I can."

He nods. "I know. But so are we."

The big tents selling TT merchandise are unrolling and securing the thick flaps and closing up shop. All the fans have retreated to their hotel rooms or campsites. People run past us holding newspapers over their heads.

"I feel like if I don't qualify, you guys are gonna … I dunno." I can't bring myself to finish the thought.

"Man, you need to give your head a shake," he says.

I look at him, surprised.

"The only one riding your ass is you," he continues.

"Make it or not, this has been nothing but amazing. For the first time in my life, I actually feel like I belong somewhere and like I can be myself and no one's pointing fingers at me." He slings an arm over my shoulders. "Scott, you've got more balls than anyone I know. Screw these podium guys, you're my friggin' hero."

I utter a laugh only because I don't know what to say. I'm kinda touched. My gut twists a bit when I think about what I did to him, putting him down in front of Branna. "Look, for what it's worth," I say, "I never thought you were the one behind the thefts at work. I even told Russ that."

"Really?" he asks.

I nod. "Yeah."

He shoves his hands into his pockets and gazes down at the ground. "Yeah, well … I was."

I pull off my helmet, letting the rain hit my head and face. "Seriously?"

He kicks a stone and we watch it bounce a few times before it rolls to a stop. "I took fifty-six bucks from John Stapleton's locker. But let's just say that by the end of the shift it had reappeared and I was sorry. And then let's just say that John never went back to Russ to mention that the money had been returned and the thefts just kept happening."

"No way."

"Yup."

"Huh," I say. "Now that you mention it, John kept talking about how he was getting his own bike and every week he'd be showing me something new he got for it: boots, gloves, leather jacket, helmet ... but if you knew it was John, why didn't you just tell Russ?"

"And what, admit I stole something the first time around? I'd have been out for sure. And you woulda kicked me out of the house."

We enter Paddock B and I have to admit he's right, and nothing Neil could've said or done would've changed my mind. "Stapleton's a shitty guy," I say.

"Yeah, well, maybe he'll get caught."

"So what made you put the money back?"

Dean shrugs. "I kept thinking about you and Neil being decent to me and giving me a chance when you didn't have to and, I dunno, it just didn't feel right."

"That's cool. Well, sorry for outing you like that in front of Branna. It was none of my business. I should have kept my mouth shut."

"Yeah, well, it gave me a chance to come clean."

"Was she mad?"

"Naw, she said she was happy that we ended up talking about it."

"That's good. I like her. The Quiggins are nice people."

"I know," he says and I realize he and I both have something in common. Missing parents.

We turn the corner to Paddock C. "Hey, you still coming out with us tomorrow?" he asks. "Watch me do the Ramsey Sprint?"

I'd forgotten about it. What I should be doing is studying the course and —

"It's my thing for Neil," he adds.

Frig, hearing him say that chokes me up and I'm kinda glad that it's raining because my eyes are getting wet. "Wouldn't miss it for the world, man."

We see Garth still in his race leathers sitting under his tent canopy. In his arms he cradles his baby as Jean cups a mug of tea.

"Hey ya," she says to us.

Dean and I wave back.

"You two look like drowned cats. Fancy a cup?" She holds up her mug.

We smile and head over to spend the rest of the afternoon with our neighbours, watching the rain pour down and trading race stories.

Dean barges into my room. "Yo, Scott," he hollers. "Get up, man. Let's go. Shakey-wakey, hands off snakey."

He grabs my pillow and swats me in the face with it, hard. "Come on, man, we're leaving for Ramsey in a half-hour. God, you stink, take a shower." He sticks his head in the hallway. "Stinky's up now," he yells and I fire the pillow back at him. He dodges it, laughs, and shuts the door behind him.

After a shower and breakfast, we load Alan's bike into the van and set out for Ramsey. Dean's mood is all over the place. One second he's bouncing around like a ten-year-old and the next he's trying to act all mellow and cool. Twenty minutes later, we arrive at the Mooragh Promenade. It's a sea of bikes and the place is packed. It's like everyone on the island's come out to watch fans run the one-eighth-mile drag strip as hard as they can. As we make our way to registration, one of the organizers hands me a program and I find out they've got classes for all types of bikes, including vintage, classic, and street legal. It looks like a lot of fun and I half-wish I was doing it.

Mags and Branna get Dean registered and join the queue for bike inspection while I spot Roger and some of the other riders who've also taken the day off to come out and watch. We shoot the breeze about the Sprint and the TT and watch a couple of the Sprint competitors whiz past us on bikes. One guy's bike shoots two-foot flames from the exhaust, making us all hoot and cheer.

Dean's class is up next so I head over to see how he's doing. He's the last of twelve to ride. He looks cool in Neil's leather jacket and Alan's helmet, but it's easy for me to see that he isn't. His face is fish-belly white.

I walk over to him. "Hey, man. How's it going?"

"Okay."

"Where're Mags and Branna?"

"Down at the other end. Branna's recording it."

"Sure you're okay?"

"Yeah, why?"

"'Cause you're doing the million-mile stare."

He presses his lips together, then licks them, which

is something my dad said I used to do whenever I got nervous.

I'm about to tell him not to sweat it, that it's no big deal. I mean, it's not like doing the TT, but then I put myself in his boots. This is his first race.

Dean bounces up and down in his seat in a useless attempt to burn off energy. I know this because I'm familiar with the move, because I *do* that move. Guy's heart's probably pounding like crazy, too.

The line of riders crawls forward as they start taking off one at a time. Dean still looks tight.

He hunches his back like he's still on the motocross bike and it takes me back to my first race when I moved up from lightweight 250s to heavier production bikes and I needed to change my riding style to maximize leverage on the handlebars.

"Hey," I say and he turns to look at me. "Uncurl your spine." He sits up and his shoulders drop and release the tension. I gently slap him on the back. "Just have fun with it, man. That's what it's all about." He nods and walks the bike toward the starters' line. Before he's on deck, I shout out one last piece of advice: "Ride like you're late for work!"

He throws his head back and laughs, then saddles up to the start. The official counts down and then he's off.

He flies down the strip, wheels spinning and kicking up a huge rooster tail of mud. Watching him makes me feel giddy and proud, like he's my kid or something. This must have been how my dad felt whenever he watched me race. By the time I jog an eighth of a mile through the crowd toward the finish line, he's standing next to the bike, helmet tucked under his arm, and sporting the biggest grin I've ever seen — molars showing and everything. Man, Neil would have loved to have seen this — good ol' Dean-er ten feet tall and having the time of his life. Goosebumps ripple across my back.

"Yes!" I cry and think, this is what being on a bike is all about. Nirvana. I give Dean a high-five. "Way to go, man."

He's smiles so hard he can't even answer. His mood's contagious because now *I* feel like I just finished the Ramsey Sprint. "So?" I finally press him. "How was it? Come on, details."

All four of our heads come together as Branna replays everything on her mini-handicam and he gives us the play-by-play. Seeing him like this, all smiles, there's nothing in the world quite like it.

One of the organizers comes over with a certificate and T-shirt that has Dean's time written on it in permanent marker. One-eighth of a mile in 7.91 seconds.

We erupt in a chorus of cheers along with a bunch of random spectators. Race fans are the best.

"Let's get our man a beer!" I shout.

"A six-pack," he adds.

"To the pub," some voice in the crowd chimes in.

We burst through the doors of the nearest two-hundred-year-old fine-ale establishment. The air's abuzz with men and women talking about their sprint runs. Every time someone comes into the place holding or wearing their T-shirt, people raise their pints in the air and shout, "Hurray!" Of course, when it happens to Dean he shouts back, "Hey! How's it going, eh?"

We pig out on queenies, and halfway through our meal I raise my water glass for a toast. "Dean, watching you today reminded me of my first race. My dad put me in the class with the older boys — they were nine and I was only six ..."

Mags and Branna look mock-shocked, playing with me as they hear the massive age difference.

"... and he said, 'Son, if it's not fun, don't do it.' Well, man, today you were great." I quickly shut the hell up because I have no idea where I'm going with that thought. It made sense in my head a few seconds ago.

"So what you're saying, Scott," Dean says, "is that I'm like a six-year-old?"

"Well," I say, "if the shoe fits . . ." We laugh, then I add, "Look, all I'm saying is that it was good to see you have fun. Neil would have loved it."

We smile, thinking of Neil, and drink. I think to myself, to hell with it. Qualify or not, I've got nothing to prove tomorrow. I've done everything I can and I'm damn happy with what I've already done, especially on a road course that takes three friggin' years to learn.

chapter 18

Sunday. Last day to qualify. Weather's decent. We hang out at the paddock. Mags and I double-check the bike and polish the fairing for something to do. Dean entertains us with his guitar and makes up a song about us racing in the TT and eating queenies. It's catchy. Arnie drops by to chat with us, and I introduce him to Garth and his family.

A stocky bald guy wearing a massive headset and orange fire-retardant overalls and holding a microphone comes over too. His friend holds a TV camera, and baldy introduces himself and asks if he can interview us. We all say sure. He holds up his microphone and the camera's green light switches on.

"I'm standing here in the paddock with Canadian —" he pronounces it Ca-neey-dee-an "— rider Scott Saunders and his team. What makes this privateer and his crew stand out is that no one here is over the age of twenty-two. That's got to be some sort of record, isn't it?" He says this rhetorically. "Can you introduce us to your team?"

I nod. "This is Maggie Chandler, Dean Conners, and Branna Quiggin." I fling an arm around them as I say their names. "We had a couple of other team members, Neil Bryant and my dad, but they couldn't make it."

I feel the strength of my friends as they move in closer.

He fires questions at us like where are you from, how long have you been racing, stuff like that. Then he asks the money-shot question.

"So do you think you'll qualify today?"

"I'd love to," I say. "All I can do is go out there and give 'er my best. Even if I don't qualify, it's been an amazing time. Riding the TT course — there's nothing like it in the world."

A crowd gathers and a couple of local kids who want to be on camera start clowning around on the road behind us. Their arms are straight out and their wrists twist pretend throttles as they make engine noises, *vrrumm-vrrumm* and *whee-eee.*

Once the interview is over and the fame wanes, it's back to the business of hurry-up-and-wait. After lunch, Dean comes over to me with hands shoved into his pockets and looking like he needs to confess something. He addresses me in a low voice.

"So, I was, you know —" he shrugs "— sketching and stuff and if you want, you can put this on your bike … or something." He pulls a decal from his pocket and it's a cartoon drawing of a beaver riding my race bike and wearing my red-and-black leathers and helmet. Its tail has a Canadian flag on it with two numbers in the red spaces that flank the maple. The numbers are 22 and 4: Neil and Dad.

"Dean," I say. "This is really cool, man. When'd you do this?"

"Last night. You like it? Branna helped me turn it into a sticker."

"Yeah, I like it. Mags, come here and look at this," I say. She gets up from her chair and comes over. "This is great," I tell him. "You should be an artist or something."

He looks like I'm feeding him a line.

"Seriously. You're like the most creative person I know. You hear a song once and you can play it, you sing, and you can obviously draw. I'm not sure about your dancing though."

He chuckles and I show Mags what he's made. Together we find a spot for it on the front of the bike, below the windshield.

Fifteen feet from the starters' line, Mags slaps me on the back twice and takes off. I roll the bike forward.

"Lack of adhesion flags at Gorselea," the startline controller hollers, and I nod. The guy ahead of me takes off.

Ten-second countdown.

Nine, eight …

Settle.

Six, five …

Breathe.

Three, two …

Fourth Lap: halfway mark on the course — move ass over for the right-hander and onto the short straight over the bridge toward Schoolhouse Corner. Glide to the right, pass Parliament Square. Left-hander out of the square, then a right at May Hill toward the sweet Mountain climb. Feel the temperature cooling — *air's getting thin.* Clip the curb on the left-hand corner, then a short straight climb to a full-bore right-hand bend leading to Ramsey hairpin — *give 'er a hard left* — 10 mph. Go into it tight, exit wide — gear *down into first, smell scorching clutch plates.*

Uphill to Waterworks, close the throttle, regain power, double right-hander — *nice, clean*. Forget the first corner apex, take it wide to the other side, and clip the apex on the second bend. Twenty-five-mile marker. Two sweeping left-handers and a short straight to Gooseneck. Pull her back on the sharp right-hand corner — *transmission's doing well*. Slip in behind the fairing, open the throttle, and fly. Sweep into the next two left-handers at 80 to 90 mph — *like sailing*. Climb one thousand feet in thirty seconds, needle's soaring, 170 mph on the Mountain Mile — *Hiya, Joey*. Slight right-hand kink, another bridge, pass the Mountain Box, head around the Verandah, aim wide on the first corner, take the second one three-quarters out in the road, accelerate hard at the apex of the third corner. Exit onto the narrow straight — *deceptively fast corner* — down a mini-straight toward Bungalow — *three-quarter mark*.

I fly past the grandstand, then pull over to the finishers' area and circle back around, up the return lane. I see my crew waiting for me, smiling.

I get off the bike feeling pretty damn good with last practice day. Mags takes over, rolling the bike alongside me as the four of us make our way through the mob. Most of the fans have gathered around the top riders' tents, so we're stuck in the crowd until marshals clear a path. Thank god for marshals. I unzip my leathers down to my waist because I'm dripping in sweat. Some random hand slaps me on the back. When we reach our paddock, I peel off my leathers and sit on the van's bumper in my blue undershirt, socks, and gitch, not caring if the girls see or not. Branna hands me my drink, which I down, then I ask Dean for his water bottle. He gives it to me and I dump it over my head.

"I just want to say that it's been great working with you guys," I say. "You've all been awesome."

"You too, brother," Dean says. Branna gives me a hug and Mags kisses me on the cheek before hugging me. Now I totally feel self-conscious in my underwear. I get changed in the van, throwing on a T-shirt and some jeans and ask someone for a piece of fruit, an orange or something. Dean takes off like a man on a mission. I wipe the water and sweat from my forehead with a towel. I've done everything I can, I think. It's out of my hands now.

I climb out of the van as Dean returns with an orange that he's peeled and quartered himself. He hands it to me with no jokes attached.

I eat and rest for a few more minutes. We agree, hands down, it's been a great week.

"Alright," I say. "Let's go see if we made it." The four of us head for the grandstand with arms around one another's shoulders to check out the electronic leader-board, along with a few hundred people. We all stand around watching the tail end of last night's TT qualifying highlights. Then the screen goes black. It remains black for a couple of minutes. There's more waiting. It's like I'm back in the holding pen, waiting for my turn to start. I can barely stand it. I might even have to take a whiz. Then a long list of racers' names appear. There are lots of murmurs and "alrights" in the crowd.

God. I can't look. I scan the graphics for the Canadian flag. Dean grabs my shoulder and points.

"Yes!" Mags shouts.

Branna claps her hands over her mouth and Dean slaps me on the back. My time's 19:59. No way! Unbelievable. Not only did I qualify, but my time's impressive. *I did it.* I actually did it.

"Friggin' eh!"

Mags and Branna both hug and kiss me, which makes the spectators think I've got quite the set-up. Eh, let them think what they want, I qualified! We whip out our camera phones and pass them to strangers so they can take our photo with the leader-board in the background. I dip Mags over my arm like they do in the movies and plant one on her lips. Then she wraps her arms around me tight.

All the way home in the van I'm riding high. Everything

I say ends with the words "I qualified." Like, "Can you pass me another bottle of water? I qualified ... Can we stop off for some queenies? I qualified." It becomes our running joke. When we approach a roundabout, Dean rolls down the van's window and yells, "He qualified! He's racing in the TT!" Cars honk their horns and bikers pump their fists in victory.

hand and I slap it with mine. "See you in the pit, man," he shouts.

The two of them back away and merge into the mob. Mags pushes the bike alongside me as the first of the riders way up at the front start taking off, one every ten seconds. I see a big camera on a crane sweep in for a close-up of the rider before pulling back up for an overhead shot as he roars away. It's just like how you see it on TV and in video games.

"This is it," I say, sitting on the bike. I put in my earplugs, secure my chinstrap, and slip on my gloves.

Mags slaps me twice on the back. "Go get 'em, Scott," she shouts. "See you in the pits." She turns to go.

"Hey, Mags?" I holler.

She looks at me over her shoulder. "Yeah?"

"Thanks."

"Sure. For what?"

"Everything."

She smiles and leaves as I walk the bike closer to the startline. Thirty more guys to go. Adrenalin rushes through my body as I get my race head on. Inside my helmet I can hear myself breathe and my heart pound. A cool breeze rolls in off the ocean and the sudden drop in temperature reminds me of the first bike run of the season, when you hit the road in the crisp spring air and everything's fresh and new. Ten more guys to go, then me. I glide slowly, steadily. Settling down, focusing, picturing the course.

"Sun spots at the Crosby," the startline controller yells, reading out the matrix board.

I roll up to the startline.

Ten, nine, eight . . .

Steady now, deep breath.

Six, five . . .

Focus.

Three, two …

Go.

Second lap, third-quarter mark — bounce over the railway tracks, slow 'er down on this left- and right-sweeping bends, roughly six klicks, make up time here, down Brandywell to a triple corner, but feels like a sweeping bend, then descend, pull back on Windy Corner — *always friggin' windy here*. Right-hander, make up time to the thirty-third-mile marker, bumpier now — *hold 'er steady* — brake hard into the right, then tight left-hand corner at Keppel Gate. Plunge down, keep on the right-hand side and aim the apex, clip that corner of the left-hand bend at Kate's Cottage, drift 'er across, road disappears below the front wheel — *I'll never get used to that* — half-mile straight. Dropping three hundred feet, push the tach into the red, aim for one-fifty, there's the Creg-ny-Baa Pub. Over to the left side, pull back on the reins, take 'er down for the corner at forty-five. Clip it, drift wide — *feels like I'm unlocking the numbers to a combination safe, everything's clicking.* Tuck in again, wring the throttle. Now roll off the power … gear down. Full throttle through Brandish Corner, top gear once more, reach for that 140 mark. Slow her slightly on the Hillberry for a right-hand uphill bend. Swing on a tight left on the rise to Cronk-ny-Mona. Up ahead, a sharp ninety-degree right-hander at Signpost Corner — *Hiya, Paul!* — downhill, medium-fast left-hand to Bedstead Corner — *watch it, bumpy here* — brake hard for the full right bend at the Nook, three-quarters of a mile left. Swing left on the steep and to Governor's Bridge — *don't rush it* — tight downhill hairpin. Nasty left-hand corner, slip the clutch, accelerate out, and onto the home stretch of Glencrutchery Road, time to roll in toward the pits …

Everything slows down, just like in the movies. The red maple leaf on Branna's overalls makes it easy for me to spot her among the other pit crew members waiting for their riders. She steps out of our pit box, positioning herself right where I need to stop, and I do, inches from her body. Mags puts the bike onto the rear stand. I relax my legs. Branna opens the gas cap. Dean inserts the fuel hose while Mags snaps off my visor and replaces it in one fluid motion. I take the drink from Branna. Fuel pumps into the tank as Dean counts. Mags moves onto the back wheel, getting ready as Branna squeegees the windshield. Everything's tight. Manoeuvres have purpose. We move as one. Thirty-second mark: Dean removes the gas hose and Branna replaces the cap, tight. They step back, Mags takes off the rear stand. I lift my feet onto the pegs as she pushes my bike for a running start. I fire it up, sparks ignite, the engine hums rough and smooth, like wet crushed velvet. I put 'er in gear and within seconds, I'm out of the pit and roaring down Glencrutchery Road, racing toward the end of the world.

On my final lap, coming back to the grandstand, I'm greeted by the waving chequered flag and I can't help but pump my fist in victory. I downshift toward the exit and come up return road toward the front of the stands. If this were a Hollywood ending, I'd spot my dad and Neil somewhere in the crowd. I know it's a silly thought, but on some level I know they're here. I pull up in front of the stands to find that more than half the fans have already left and are in the paddock, securing prime positions for autographs from the top riders, who finished the race fifteen minutes ago. Incredibly, the podium ceremony is over. The champagne has been shaken, uncorked, and sprayed. The silver trophy, fashioned after the Olympic God Hermes, has already been held high and kissed by the winner. The top three guys are all in the press office for more photo ops. I am by no means the last guy to finish, but it just goes to show how fast the pros really are.

There's still a crowd of people welcoming us home though, cheering and clapping, including my friends. I stop the bike in front of them, cut the engine, climb off, and hug them. They're just as happy as I am, even though they mock-choke at being covered in bugs.

I remove my helmet and look up at the twenty-foot-high podium where the winners had stood only moments ago.

"Go on!" a voice shouts to us from the stands. I look over and see that it's Paul and he's saying exactly what I'm thinking.

"Follow me," I say to Mags, Dean, and Branna. Two guys from Arnie's crew who happen to be walking by offer to hold my bike. We hike up the podium stairs, the metal underfoot sticky from victory booze. When we reach the top, the view is spectacular. We raise our fists in the air, imagining glory, and cry out like we've won one of the TT races. People whistle and clap for us.

It's like I said, race fans are the best. Our photographer, 167, sees us and snaps our photo. "That's the real photo op!" he cries.

Mags smiles at me and I hand Dean my helmet so I can place my hands on either side of her face and kiss her in one of those smooches that tells everyone I think she's the hottest woman here. A couple of people in the crowd cheer and whistle.

"Wha-aat?" Dean cries, he's clearly stupefied by what he's seeing.

"Oh, come on, Dean," Branna says. "It was completely obvious."

We keep kissing.

We celebrate back at the farm with a barbecue. Mags, Dean, Branna, and I raise our glasses to a job well done, then to Neil and my dad. We don't need to say a thing. We've been amazing. I'm so stoked I ended up with a time of 19:36, I could friggin' cry. I take my first swig of beer in a long time and it goes down smooth.

Alan and Gwen come out of the house with lamb chops for the grill, and Pickles circles around Dean, her tail doing the cha-cha. Dean's going to miss that dog, I think. We all take our seats at the picnic table.

"So does this mean you'll be coming back next year?" Alan asks.

"For sure," I say. "Well, if my team will have me and doesn't upgrade riders first."

Mags kicks me under the table.

"I'm going to go for sponsorship next year," I add "so I can enter the superstock and the superbike classes, too."

"Well, I guess you'll see me here when you get back," Dean says.

Mags and I look over at him at the same time.

He grins. "Gwen and Alan offered me a job on the farm."

"Really? That's awesome," I say and Mags nods, agreeing with me. "Guess I'll have a free room to crash in when I come back."

Dean chuckles. "Actually, they're making me sleep in the barn."

"That's a great idea," Alan says and Gwen laughs.

"Hey, do you mind storing my stuff at your place for a while?" Dean asks.

I shrug like it's no big deal. "Sure."

"So what's next when you get home, Scott?" Alan wants to know.

"Aside from selling Dean's stuff? I was thinking of doing the eight-hour Endurance Race in Cape Town, South Africa, in December."

"That sounds fantastic," he says.

I turn to Mags, "Up for joining me?"

She jokes by making like she's not sure, then a smile spreads across her face. "I think I can do that. But I'd have to see about school though."

"Wait, I thought you were done with school," I say.

She helps herself to a lamb chop. "Arnie and I have been talking and I've decided to go back, but I'm switching majors — I'm going into mechanical engineering."

"That's cool. Makes sense," I say.

"Yeah, and Arnie says that when I graduate, I'll have a job on his team."

I look into her smiling green eyes. I couldn't be happier for her. It's what she's always wanted. I raise my glass in her honour and fall for her all over again.

After dinner, as Dean helps the Quiggins clean up, Mags and I go for a walk along the train tracks. I take her hand in mine and kiss the back of it. I don't know if this means we're a couple or not, but I'm just enjoying it for what it is.

"So, do you think Dean'll be okay?" she asks.

"Definitely. I think getting the hell out of Ferber is the best thing for him. I'm happy for the guy."

"Yeah, me too." Mags squeezes my hand. "Um . . . hey, there's something I wanted to tell you earlier ... but I couldn't get you on your own."

"What?"

We stop walking and she takes a deep breath and I wonder if I should brace myself for some bad news.

"Terry passes along his congratulations," she says.

"Terry?" I echo.

She nods.

"Did he call or something?"

Mags shakes her head. "No. We've been in contact by email since I got here. He's been following you on-line all week."

I let go of her hand. "Why didn't you say anything?"

"I would have told you, but he made me swear not to. He thought you had enough on your mind without hearing from him."

I shrug. "I don't know about that." My gut tightens at the thought of things still not being right, and I remember back to what she'd said in the van the day I broke down on the course. "Mags? Do you remember when you asked me if I knew why Terry didn't come around to see me?"

She nods as if clearly remembering that day in the van too. "Yeah."

"Does he blame himself for what happened to my dad? Because he shouldn't. It wasn't his fault. The investigation concluded that it was neither driver nor mechanical error, but a sudden failure that happened without warning."

She takes both of my hands in hers. "Have you told him that? Maybe you should. He's never outright said it, but ..." Her voice trails off.

It all makes sense now, why he never comes around

and why he can't look me in the eye. He thinks he killed his best friend. I sigh, thinking about the burden he must be carrying.

For the rest of race week we watch the superbike, superstock, lightweight, and sidecar races from various locations around the course, like Bray Hill and Cronk-y-Voddy, and from people's yards like at Harold's Garden and Signpost Corner. I'm definitely stoked to secure some heavy-duty sponsorship next year so I can participate in more classes.

Between races, I help break down and drain the fluids from my bike to ship it out, and Mags spends a lot of time at the paddock with Arnie and his crew getting more work experience under her belt. On the final night of the last race, we all get cleaned up and dressed for the awards dinner at the theatre in Douglas. It basically means taking a shower and putting on clean jeans. It's a dinner where they call riders up to the stage and award silver and bronze replicas of the Hermes trophy to the fastest riders and finishers' medals to the rest of us. It's considered quite an achievement to even finish the TT, so to receive a medal means a lot. Since there are only four of us sitting at a table that normally holds ten, Arnie and his crew invite us to join their two tables. When it's my turn to go up on stage, I get the surprise of my life when the MC announces that I'm also this year's fastest newcomer.

I'm so blown away by this, I barely hear the crowd cheering.

We celebrate with beers and later, a drunken stroll along the prom. Dean and I dare each other to ride The Vomitnator. I like to think that we don't because we're too wasted and don't want to upchuck, mid-air, but the girls say it's because we're chicken and to prove us wrong, they go for a spin.

Gwen said that the Isle of Man has a way of working into your bones and she was right. I can't believe how three weeks have blown by so fast. One second all three of us are piling off the ferry in the fog and rain and the next, Dean and Branna are giving Mags and me a lift back to the terminal.

Riding in the front of the van next to Mags, I squeeze her hand and she squeezes mine back. I'm guessing this means we're together now, but we haven't talked about it officially, so I'm just going to enjoy it in the moment for what it is.

I glance out the window as Branna takes us along the promenade. The fun fair is slowly being dismantled and ahead of us a few hundred motorcycle riders, saddled with backpacks and camping gear, drive toward the ferry. They came from all over Europe to be here, and I figure it'll take some of them another week's worth of driving to reach home.

Out at sea, about a third of a mile from shore on a partially submerged reef, I see the mini-castle that's featured on a lot of postcards and souvenirs. At the top of the structure, the Isle of Man flag flaps in the wind, red background and three armoured legs with golden spurs, "whichever way you throw us, we always land on our feet." It's a good motto for life, I think.

Branna finds a parking spot and we pile out. Seagulls cry overhead as ferry workers direct drivers and bikers to board in an orderly fashion. Since everyone hates long, drawn-out goodbyes that just get filled with awkward small talk, I just go for it and start. I extend my hand to the guy I now consider a good friend.

"Well, see ya, man," I say to him. "Take it easy, eh?"

He steps forward and gives me a hug and a manly slap on the back. "You too."

I smile. I actually think I'm going to miss the guy. I give Branna a big hug and whisper, "Take care of him, will you?"

"I will," she whispers back.

With our gear in tow, Mags and I make for the passenger boarding plank and turn around for one final wave.

The next day when our plane lands in Toronto at 6 a.m., Mags sits and waits with me in the departure area for my flight to Vancouver. She's going to stay in Toronto to meet up and talk with her folks and to sort out the school situation. I wonder if it'll mean that she has to move back and go to school there, or if she'll be able go to school out in BC.

She lays her head on my shoulder and we lean against each other, exhausted.

"So guess what Terry said when I gave him my notice?" she says in a sleepy voice.

I take her hand and trace the calluses on her fingers and palm with my thumb. "I'm thinking he said it was only a matter of time before you moved on."

She nods. "Pretty much."

"Well, it's true," I say.

"He's a good guy. Best boss I ever had." I give her hand a squeeze and close my eyes. Her warm breath feels nice on my neck.

We both must have nodded off because the pre-boarding announcement wakes us up. I open my eyes to see passengers already lined up with tickets at the ready for flight staff inspection. I look at Mags and her pretty brown eyes and now wish I hadn't slept.

I hoist myself up from the seat and extend my hand to help her out of hers. We join the back of the queue. I wrap my arm around her; she leans into me.

"It's going to be weird going home to an empty house," I say. I think back to what Paul said the first day we met going around the TT course, how he was saying hello to old friends. "You know what I was thinking of doing?" I add. "I want to invite a bunch of people over and plant a tree in the backyard to remember my dad and Neil."

We move forward with the crowd. "I think that's a great idea," she says. "I want to be there. Can you wait for me? I'll be back next week."

I kiss her on the forehead. "Call me and I'll pick you up from the airport," I tell her.

"Thanks. So, hey, I was thinking about driving across the country on my bike with my stuff this summer.

Would you be up for a road trip?"

I throw my hands out at my sides. "Hell yeah. Gotta train for Cape Town, don't I?"

She gives me a hug and before it's my turn to board, we kiss goodbye, and when our lips part I suddenly wish for next week to get here — now.

I hand my ticket to the airline agent, who scans it.

"I hope you don't mind," Mags says, walking backwards, away from me, "but I arranged a little something for you."

"What's that?"

"You'll see." She blows me a kiss and waves, and I disappear down the loading ramp.

When I land in Vancouver just shy of five hours later, I shoulder my carry-on and make my way to the baggage claim area. After I'm cleared by customs, I head down a long tunnel toward two oversize automatic doors leading to the arrivals area. The doors slide open and a few hundred people stand looking expectantly for someone other than me.

I head for the exit when I spot a familiar face in the crowd, smiling.

Terry.

acknowledgements

I owe a big debt of gratitude to a lot of people for helping me accomplish this ambitious project. Thank you to Simon Crellin and the TT organizers for believing in my story and granting me press passes over the years. Thank you to my agent, Rebecca Friedman, for taking a chance on me, and thank you to my editor, Carrie Gleason, for caring about good books.

Thank you to all those who openly shared their racing stories and TT adventures: newcomers, privateers, veterans, podium champs, travelling marshals, pit crew, mechanics, scrutineers, organizers, Supporters Club, TT Marshals' Association, volunteer marshals, journalists, film and TV crews, photographers, homestay families, Islanders, and, of course, the die-hard TT race fans. Thank you to Nick Jefferies, John McBride, Brandon Cretu, Charlie

Lambert, Peter Causer, Stephen Davison, John Skinner, Michelle Duff, Pat Barnes, Graeme McDonough, Kevin Ago Murphy, and Gilli Pires for offering your racers' insights and answering ten million questions.

Thank you to my friends, family, the folks at Wildacres, and the Nachos and Narratives (Stephen Geigen-Miller, Claire Humphrey, Greg Beettam, Sean Davidson), who provided such generous and enthusiastic feedback and support.